the FRISIAN

Richard van der Ven

FIRST STEPS PUBLISHING

The Frisian, The Legacy of Willibrord
A Medieval Quest of Betrayal, Vengeance and Glory
by Richard van der Ven

Copyright © 2023 by Richard van der Ven
All rights reserved., First Edition © January 2024

Published by First Steps Publishing, Gleneden Beach, Oregon 97388

ISBN-13:
   978-1-944072-91-9 (hc)
   978-1-944072-90-2 (pbk)
   978-1-944072-92-6 (epub)

Thank you for buying an authorized edition of this book.

NO AI TRAINING: Without in any way limiting the author's [and publisher's] exclusive rights under copyright, any use of this publication to "train" generative artificial intelligence (AI) technologies to generate text is expressly prohibited. The author reserves all rights to license uses of this work for generative AI training and development of machine learning language models.

Without limiting the rights under copyright, no part of this publication may be reproduced, stored in or introduced into a retrieval system, or transmitted, in any form, or by any means (electronic, mechanical, photocopying, recording, or otherwise), without the prior written permission of both the copyright owner and the above publisher of this book.

PUBLISHING NOTE: This is a book of fiction. Names, characters, places and incidents either are the product of the author's imagination or are used fictitiously, and any resemblance to actual persons (living or dead), businesses, companies, events or locales is entirely coincidental. Every effort has been made to be accurate. The publisher assumes no responsibility or liability for errors made in this book.

Cover layout, book layout & design by Suzanne Parrott
Map design, interior graphics, Cover art: *The Frisian*, © 2023 Suzanne Parrott

Printed and bound
in the United States of America.

RichardVanDerVen.com

To my father

Frisia

North Sea

The Kingdom of England

- Rhuddlan
- Richard's Castle (Hereford)
- Friston
- Hereford
- Ipswich
- London

- Starum
- Veenkoop
- Wiltenburg
- Thuredrith

English Channel

The Frisian
1055

Chapter One

I woke, shaking from the cold. I felt my clothes instinctively, stroking the long white shirt I wore in bed. Damp again. Blinking, I slowly rose. As the morning sun began to peek through the window, the room gradually filled with soft, warm light, casting a gentle glow on the bed. Thinking back to last night, my lips curled up at the thought of Gerda shedding her clothes in the stables. Certainly, an evening to remember.

Yawning, I glanced at our banner on the wall above the fireplace. It displayed two silver fish on a blue background, our coat of arms. The sunlight brought out the richness and depth of the hues, almost allowing the fish to swim in the endless aquamarine of the banner. It made me squint, my eyes gradually adjusting to the brightness around me.

Whispering a morning prayer, I felt a few drops of water land on my head. I glanced up to notice the ceiling had a small leak, likely caused by the storm that had raged through the area a few days ago. Despite the damage, I felt hope wash over me as I prayed. The rain outside had stopped, and the sky was clear, a sign of better things.

My name, Reginhard, was bestowed upon me by my father, a proud Frisian from our wild and rugged coast. Born and raised in these damp and marshy lowlands, I spent most of my childhood amidst the harsh elements of the western coast. The salty sea air and relentless winds shaped me into a strong and resilient young man as I learned to navigate the treacherous peatlands of my home.

My father initially got sent to the region by the ruler of the Holy Roman Empire, Henry III, to punish the rebellious Count Dirk of Frisia, whom he then shot in battle with an arrow. Because of his excellent service, Father was awarded a ministerial appointment, after which he built a sturdy hoeve, a Frisian manor house.

I snorted as I reflected on the irony. Truly the most comfortable home imaginable. Comfortable and cold and as wet as the floods from Noah's time.

A grating voice broke my inner reflections, piercing the soft whispering of the wind. 'You're awake. Good,' Father grunted as he appeared in the doorway to face me, his brow furrowed. 'I want you to accompany Ome Aitet and help him fix the northern dyke before you join Jan's expedition this afternoon.' I bit my lip. So now I had to repair what any damn peasant could do in his sleep while I should be joining the expedition in Thuredrith. What was Father thinking? My brother was already in the Castellan's personal guard while I had to strut around the bloody dykes. I hated this boring life at the estate. Still, I dared not look my father in the eye. I knew exactly what followed whenever I didn't heed his commands.

'Why, what's wrong with it?' I replied, still half asleep. The construction of this brand-new wall was completed only two weeks ago. Was it broken already?

As I blinked again, trying to wake up properly, Ome Aitet, the estate's overseer, now strolled in. 'Come on, put your tunic on lad!' He boomed in his usual lively manner. He glanced at Father, his eyes beaming. 'Good morning Lord Salaco.'

Father greeted his overseer, then, growing impatient with my sluggish morning ritual, kicked me into action. 'Come on now. You must learn how to manage an estate as well as wield a sword. Overseeing your own land will determine your survival later.'

Realising I moved ever closer to one of Father's familiar thrashings, I quickly pulled a sheepskin over my tunic, the soft fur emanating a soothing warmth over my chest. Sheepskins provided much-needed protection from the biting winds on these early spring mornings, as the thick wool kept me warm even in the coldest temperatures.

Mother then moved in from the cooking area to hand me a piece of dark bread, still warm from the oven. I thanked her, savouring the rich, nutty flavor, before putting on my leather boots. Then, wasting no more time, I rushed out to meet Ome Aitet, passing Father, who stood stone-faced in the corner.

Once outside, I noticed the overseer pacing back and forth, his energy evident in every step. I could tell he was eager to get the repairs done. A man of simple farming stock, he was of average height with dark, greying hair of medium length. He wore a simple sheepskin cloak over wide braies and leather boots of decent quality, allowing him to trudge effectively through the peat around us.

The estate was filled with two dozen sheep grazing in grasslands hemmed in by sturdy dykes that protected us from floods. I smirked. Only nine years ago, our estate was nothing but the marshy bank of a tributary to the Thure River, ending up in the rough seas that bordered this newly cleared area. Yet now, the place is settled not only by animals but also by a village of colonists from Wiltenburg. We christened this cluster of humble huts encircling the manor Veenkoop, which was under the ministerial leadership of my father.

Our entire estate included this village, our hoeve, – the hall where my family lived – a tithe barn to store the produce, a large barn for storing our agrarian tools, and a small stable with four decent enough horses. We also created a dirt road linking our demesne to the town of Thuredrith, allowing us to move our produced goods there.

I held my breath when I passed the dung heap on the edge of Veenkoop; then, I inhaled deeply, enjoying the salty, fresh air and an expansive, watery view. I shuddered as the river pounded against the high dykes in the distance.

Not a week ago, Veenkoop suffered a storm that lasted for days on end, every instance of which we feared for our lives. Yet that was nothing new; the rivers often slammed against the mud walls that fought to keep us all dry. At times, water penetrated nature's defences, as had happened to the northern dyke, when a deluge poured directly into our fields. I sighed deeply. This flood now threatened to undo months of land clearing. We had to act fast and repair the breach so no more water could stream into the field.

Rays of sunlight pierced through the clouds as we reached our destination and found the broken dyke wall. Ome Aitet scanned the field, his hand covering his eyes. 'No grain will grow here for quite a while lad.' He tasted the flood water. 'Brackish, as I feared. Only sheep can graze here for now.'

'Will we ever be able to grow anything here?' I wondered aloud.

'Only if we can strengthen the walls so they won't break anymore, allowing the soil to gradually become less saline.' Ome Aitet pointed at the damaged wall, where the earth had crumbled under the weight of the river's water. 'The rising river put too much pressure on the wall and it overflowed there – at its weakest point.'

'But why did it break?' I asked as I gazed towards the shattered dyke. It was new; it should have held.

Ome Aitet grunted, furiously shaking his head. 'Gerold reinforced that section.'

Gerold mainly herded our sheep, his best friends, apparently. Since every peasant helped whenever dykes were built or repaired, Gerold had tried to do his part. Here, he had obviously failed us. I sighed. 'Better he just tend to the sheep then.'

'Well, whatever he did, we have to fix it now, so better get to it. Let's round up the men and clear out the water', Ome Aitet decided promptly.

I nodded, feeling a new surge of energy. I wanted nothing else than to get going. Frethirik's father was waiting for me in Thuredrith, and I promised to get to him before noon. 'I'll ask Gerold to get the farmers.'

'Five will do, plus Gerold himself. Then let the brainless bugger tend to the sheep after he's done. That, at least, he can do, the idiot.'

Ome Aitet began to shovel the loose earth back onto the wall. 'Bloody hell, I was supposed to hunt some hares for your father today.'

As I sprinted back to the village, my mind just couldn't let go of the coming adventure. The excitement of it pushed me forward like a wolf on the hunt. The thought of the thrill that awaited me and Frethirik was almost too much to bear. 'Let's finish this business quickly then,' I mumbled. 'I hate all this boring farm work.'

After ordering the peasants to assemble in front of the manor, I returned with some spirited lads in tow, the urgency of the situation clear to all. The broken wall loomed ahead of us, a gaping hole threatening to flood the entire peat field. But the men, undaunted, rushed to Ome Aitet's side, shoveling water away from the wall with a frenzy to match.

They dug canals to redirect the surplus water, their muscles straining with effort. As the channels took shape and the water began to recede from the field, their contented sighs instilled hope in a good outcome. The sun broke from the clouds again, the men now grinning in satisfaction; they knew they had beaten the water.

This is all taking too long, I thought, my impatience growing. 'I really want to get going,' I muttered as Ome Aitet directed some men to repair the wall. He shook his head at Gerold, who stared at the sheep with a blank expression. 'Gerold, focus,' he said, his brow furrowing. 'We need to repair this wall properly, or it will fail when the next storm comes.'

Ome Aitet showed him how to mix the mud and apply it to the damaged section of the wall. 'Don't just shovel the mud on the wall. Remember what you father taught you lad. Make sure you add enough water to the mud,' he instructed. 'It needs to be sticky enough to hold together, but not so wet that it will slide off the wall.'

As Gerold began to work on the wall, Ome Aitet moved on to direct the other men. They worked quickly, their hands and feet caked in mud as they built up the damaged section of the dyke.

Since I trusted Ome Aitet to oversee the repairs, I turned around to look at the sun. How long before noon? And just then, I heard a familiar tune from the direction of the village. A sturdy, red-faced young man with blond hair, whistling an old Frisian melody, strolled into view, wearing a warm smile. His approach put a smirk on my face, and I couldn't help but mumble out loud, 'Finally, thank God.' Frethirik was probably sent to pick me up, releasing me from this distasteful chore.

'Good morning Reginhard,' he greeted me. 'I thought we agreed to meet in Thuredrith before noon.' He pointed at the sun. 'Or has your father ruined your day again, commanding you to farm labour?'

I punched him on the shoulder. 'I am overseeing the farmers, Frethirik, not labouring myself.'

'Yeah whatever you tell yourself when you go to sleep Reginhard.' He shrugged. 'Shall we go then? Father told me we really had to hurry up, or he will sail without us.' I nodded, glancing at Ome Aitet.

Frethirik was one of the few people who made this harsh life better. Years ago, Father had befriended Jan Ubbeson, Frethirik's father, a half-Frisian, half-Dane, who commanded a longboat manned by forty warriors. Famous as a notorious pirate praying on Flemish merchant vessels, he also proved a valuable mercenary to various lords in Frisia. At present, he made his living in service of the Castellan of Thuredrith, bringing back any spoils he took from merchants to be divided between them. 'A win-win situation,' he always told us at the firepit.

Over the years, my father saw a profitable agreement grow and even joined Jan on various expeditions. Through these ventures, Father had acquired an extra mail hauberk and a longsword for his second child, me, not at all a regularity for a ministerial's second son. And God, was I proud of that suit of armour.

So, since Frethirik's mother died when he was born, and his father was away sailing, Frethirik was mainly in my family's care, training day in and day out with me, tutored by my father and older brother.

I jumped up at Frethirik's remark, tugging Ome Aitet's sleeve. I stood about to plead, but the old overseer already nodded, not interested in whether we stayed or moved on.

My father often remarked how much effort it took to secure a future for me and my older pig of a brother. He always foresaw that one of us had to leave at some point due to the poverty of his estate.

In fact, I had long been told that my brother would inherit the estate and I would go into the service of the bishop, something I trained for my entire life. And that training would now be put into action right before my eighteenth birthday, on our first expedition to sea.

After racing back to the hoeve, our servant stood ready to assist me with my gear. 'Lord Salaco ordered me to fetch the horses, young sirs.' As he helped me slide into the heavy mail hauberk, its iron protection reaching all the way to my knees, Frethirik grinned.

'You sure you are up to the task Reginhard? Not easy for a land rot to fight on the water you know.'

That immediately soured my mood. What did he know about fighting? He only occasionally joined his father on a trading venture, never having seen any action either.

'Hehe,' Frethirik boasted. 'We all have jobs to do, Reginhard – your lot farms and my lot sails.'

I squinted my annoyance at the arrogant bastard. 'Is that's why you never hump no girls, Frethirik, because your crew is too busy wetting your arse?'

I ducked, his fist missing me by an inch. 'That's not true,' he shouted. 'You're just lucky your father has this estate. That's the sole reason Gerda has any interest in you anyway, you spoiled prick.'

His furrowed brow made me smile, and I couldn't help adding, 'you could always invite Gerold into your bed, he looks at you funny every time you walk past.' By now, my smile had reached my ears. 'And maybe he wants a good hump too, heh!'

Before I could even blink, a rock hurtled towards my face. I dodged to the side, only just avoiding it. I glanced over at my friend, still grinning at him. Despite the anger of his throw, he suddenly burst into a tirade of laughter, and I joined in immediately. It was just how we were together – always teasing each other, finding humour in the most unexpected moments. But all jokes aside, we now stood ready to embark on our adventure, a journey that would first take us to Thuredrith, some five and a half miles away.

Chapter Two

 Contemplating the adventure that awaited us, we rode in silence toward Thuredrith. The first noticeable landmark to pass was Ome Aitet's hut, which stood at the fork of two side rivers of the Thure on the northeastern edge of my father's demesne. It was nothing special, just a simple wooden hut, but Ome Aitet had built it on a small mound there, something the Frisians call a terp, which protected him from floods. He had also made his own little ferry – no more than a raft– which he could use to pass the river whenever he fished in the area.

 After crossing a wooden bridge, the dirt road led us towards Thuredrith's western woods, where a pair of house sparrows sang their melodies, encouraging us to join in with an ancient Frisian battle song. Sunlight shone through the branches to light up our faces, warming my mood even more. A few miles on, we entered the vast expanse of Thuredrith's surroundings, with flat grasslands as far as the eye could see. In the distance stood the town itself, its details slowly emerging.

 Thuredrith stood tall in these lowlands, built upon raised earthworks and topped by wooden palisade walls. Massive banners on each side of the gate, showing the colours red and white, welcomed those who neared its entrance. A few guards could be seen on the battlements while two sullen young townsmen stood by the gate. One was round like a barrel, the other as slender as a twig. They were dressed in simple brown tunics, each holding a spear and a shield with the town's colours on display.

The twig squinted as we neared. 'Reginhard, Frethirik, welcome back.' He let us through with a careless movement of his spear. We rode side by side through the wide entrance of the town, the road leading into a bustling fairground. We passed several huts and small merchant establishments, staring up as we always did at the keep that housed the castellan, the most powerful man in the area. I wondered what my brother was doing at this very moment, probably standing guard in one of the rooms. I glanced at Frethirik. 'God, how I wish for a keep like that. See how high it stands, and how much larger than my father's manor.'

My friend shrugged. 'I just want silver and men to follow me in battle. Well, a nice place to live too I guess. Yet I do not care for these Frankish towers.'

I chuckled. Like a true Frisian, my friend always clung to our forefathers' old beliefs. He had a strong connection with this Frisian heritage, often leading to disagreements and misunderstandings. Like my father, I hung much more towards the Frankish ways, my goal above all to gain an estate of my own. Still, despite our different views, I knew Frethirik as a loyal comrade with his heart in the right place, and I valued our friendship beyond anything else.

Having reached the fairground, the road became too crowded, so we dismounted. Grabbing the horses by the reins, we walked through the marketplace, taking in its sights and sounds. Vendors shouted out their wares, enticing customers to their stalls. Some sold fresh fruits and vegetables, offering baked bread and pastries, while others displayed meat or poultry. The smell of fresh food mingled with the strong smell of fish, with the sour stink of the open sewage and waste spread throughout the town floor.

The market bustled with activity as the townspeople haggled with vendors, shaking hands or screaming sharp objections whenever a price proved too high. The ground in front of the wooden stalls was littered with straw and sawdust, a welcome home to stray dogs and rats that searched the area for food. Dogs whined at vendors, begging for scraps, while the rats peeked out of holes in the wooden structures, waiting for their moment. Despite these unsanitary conditions, this fairground had become a vital hub of commerce and trade over the years, turning Thuredrith into a thriving town.

We trudged deeper into the market, spotting several merchants selling exotic spices, herbs, and perfumes while others displayed precious stones and metals. Street performers took center stage, entertaining the crowds with music, acrobatics, and comedy. We pushed through the crowd, forcefully moving aside anyone obstructing our path. We were warriors, and we demanded respect from these commoners.

But the over-eager performers just kept dancing in front of our feet. Gritting my teeth, I bashed my shoulder into a musician, causing his cup full of clinking coins to spill onto the ground. Without a second glance, we proceeded into the refreshing open air of the harbour, where the mighty Thure River allowed a fresh wind to greet us, blowing the putrid air of the market back into the heart of town.

As we approached the riverfront, many ships of all sizes and shapes moored there, from small fishing boats to large cargo ships. These sturdy wooden vessels could withstand the harsh conditions of the sea, most equipped with a single mast and a square sail. Frethirik pointed at a large cog, a cargo ship. 'I bet that one can transport as many as fifty men, Reginhard, and a good amount of cargo too.'

I shrugged, captivated by dock workers loading and unloading assorted goods – textiles, spices, timber, and fish. Several seafarers hoisted heavy crates and barrels onto a ship while others mended the sail and rigging. They were probably about to start another journey, I thought.

We then passed some shipyards where builders constructed and repaired different types of ships, the sounds of hammering and sawing filling my ears. I nodded to them, knowing these skilled craftsmen worked tirelessly to maintain the vital crafts that drove Thuredrith's thriving markets.

So focused on all these sights, I failed to notice a colossal warrior, broad as a barrel, blocking my path. Bumping straight into him, the giant grinned, revealing some missing teeth. 'What's this pile of rags here? You give us a girl for the boredom, Cap'n?'

'Yes, Rurik.' Frethirik's father, Jan, emerged from the hull of his ship, his confident stride and weathered face revealing his many years at sea. A towering figure with salt-and-pepper hair, his blue eyes pierced right through me. He smiled at his men, his gruff voice loud and clear. 'This here lass will learn how to fight properly and is joining our expedition to grow some balls. Along with that boy of mine.'

As Jan spoke, excitement and nervousness stirred within me. I had always dreamed of going on an adventure, and now it was happening. I felt a little scared, both of the warriors on the ship and the perils of the sea. I shook my head, straightening my back as I met Jan's gaze. I was ready to prove myself.

Forty veteran warriors now looked down at me, their eyes twinkling as they taunted me with names like 'mother's boy,' 'tiny lass,' and 'little twig.' Even Frethirik couldn't help but laugh at their jokes. I tried to brush off their teasing and made my way onto

Jan's ship, but by then, I felt a bit disheartened. This wasn't exactly the start of the adventure I had dreamed of for so long.

As I looked around the ship, I noticed several kegs of ale, sacks of hard bread, and barrels of dried fish being loaded into the hold.

'You like it?' Jan asked.

The question caught me off guard. I turned to face him, a little surprised by his sudden interest in my opinion.

'Yes, I do like it,' I replied as I kept scanning my surroundings. Despite the teasing and the rough start to the journey, there was something undeniably captivating about this ship. The intricate carvings, powerful oars, sails billowing in the wind – it was beautiful.

'It's a marvel to behold Jan. But, are you sure it will not sink when we are out at sea?' I wondered with some suspicion. 'It seems to be so low in the water?'

Jan just shook his head. 'Frethirik, why don't you explain to your friend here what the difference is between that toy you sail through your tiny rivers and this beauty?'

'It's the planks, see?' Frethirik started. 'My small boat is basically a log that my father had given me.' He made a hacking motion. 'Together with Trollmann,' he pointed at a savage-looking heathen in the ship. 'I hacked out a part of it until it was hollow and then it just basically floats and I could steer it.'

'It took a bit more than that,' Trollmann assured us, standing at the stern. As I locked eyes with this man, I was taken aback by his strange appearance. He had a lean build, with tanned skin from years spent under the sun. His dark, unkempt hair fell past his shoulders, framing a malicious grin, while a black beard with some patches of grey in it covered his chin.

As I inspected him further, I noticed he wore numerous

armrings, each bearing a story of his battles. A fur-lined coat stretched from his shoulders to his knees, almost like my iron hauberk. Over it, a white fox skin adorned his shoulders, its dark eyes staring at us, almost as if its spirit was guarding this strange man. On his red belt hung a seax and a savage-looking dagger. I could tell by how he carried himself that he was an experienced warrior, and I had no doubt that he could do terrible damage with those weapons. As he stared back at me, I quickly lowered my eyes. This Trollmann was imposing, and I started to feel uneasy around him.

Yet Frethirik rolled his eyes at him, ignoring the savage completely. 'This grand beast,' he said, gesturing to the ship, 'uses much more sophisticated techniques to keep it afloat and maneuverable. We call it a snekkja, like a snake on the water.' He then pointed at the planks. 'They overlap, see, and building like that is called clinking.'

Far from finished, Frethirik gestured to another ship built nearby, quite different from Jan's. 'Thuredrith also uses that technique to construct these cogs there for trading.' I watched how four sweating men sawed through rough logs of timber while one of them attached the overlapping planks with heavy iron nails. Although shipbuilding was not my expertise, I was impressed by the fine craftsmanship necessary to create these magnificent vessels.

As Frethirik blabbered on, I started exploring the ship, my eyes drawn to the mighty unrolled sail attached to the tall mast. I imagined what it would be like out at sea with the wind filling the sail, propelling us forward. I leaned over the railing, noticing many shields adorning the side of the ship, most in the colours of Jan's signature – simple horizontal layers of blue and white, with a golden star in the top left corner.

'That's my mum,' Frethirik explained as he touched the star on one shield, his eyes watery. 'She will guide us at sea.'

When the crew finished loading the last of the supplies, Jan's booming voice tore through our conversation. 'All right, we're all set,' he announced. 'Let's sail and rob the bloody Flemish of their silver!'

The men cheered, quickly moving to their seats. Frethirik patted my back, pointing to an empty bench. 'Come on Reginhard. We need to sit there. Now you'll really feel like a member of the crew.' He threw me on the seat. 'Grab that oar and start rotating.' It didn't take me long to understand the movement. Frethirik grinned. 'Just like that, you landrot. You're getting the hang of it now.'

We rowed out of the harbour and onto the open sea, my heart beating faster as I attuned to the crew's rhythm. The wind filled the sail, sending us flying, with the water splashing against the sides of the snekkja. This was it then, my first true adventure. The excitement rushed through my veins when I looked back, the familiar harbour of Thuredrith steadily disappearing into the distance. The Flemish better be ready for us.

Chapter Three

The next three weeks were worse than Father's harshest punishment. No experience in my entire life had been as gruesome as this excursion. Rough and cold, with constant rain, my home felt like paradise compared to this horrific trip. As the early morning sun rose over the horizon, my stomach churned with discomfort. I placed my hand over my belly, praying everything would remain intact.

I stumbled over to the side of the boat, my hand clasped over my mouth, desperately trying to hold back the bile rising in my throat. I just couldn't control it any longer, my body forcing me to expel a light-brown substance over the side of the boat. The foul smell of vomit and the salty sea air made me even more nauseous. It reminded me of the stale bread and sour beer I had consumed earlier, foolishly thinking I could handle it. Standing there, feeling weak and embarrassed, it felt as if the sea was punishing me for my earlier arrogance. I just wasn't built for this seafaring. Please just put me on a horse soon, I thought, as I grasped the silver cross hanging on my neck.

A voice broke through my aching head, nearly making it crack. 'Here, have some of this. It will help.' The cup's contents looked like my recent gift to the sea and didn't smell much better.

'Thank you, Trollmann,' I groaned. 'Is this some magic concoction you learned to brew as a Sami?' I added. Frethirik had told me that Trollmann belonged to a tribe from the furthest reaches of the kingdom of Norway called the Sami. 'Barbarians,' the Thuredrith priest would say. 'Heathens.'

Yet, to be fair, he was the only one who treated me half-decent here, other than Frethirik, of course. The crew believed he always knew what the gods wanted, so they often sought his guidance. His reputation as a powerful sorcerer was known far and wide, and many people came to him seeking blessings and protection. Yet despite his great powers, I had quickly come to know him as a humble and wise man, always using his abilities for the greater good of the crew.

'When we board that Flemish ship yonder, young lass, you need to strip off that iron vest,' he advised me, ignoring my question.

I winced. 'Take of my armour?' How could anyone suggest something so absurd? 'Why?' I frowned. 'A warrior is supposed to fight in his full armour, is he not?'

Trollmann's eyes widened. 'Well, you are a tiny little lass that has never been in any fight before,' he began, 'and that thing weighs about twice as much as you do.' His blunt tone left no room for argument, so I decided not to reply, instead folding my arms. I just couldn't believe these warriors would attack without wearing their mail. Never before had I heard anything like this from Father. Had he ever stripped of his armour at sea? Maybe Trollmann was right, I thought, looking down at the water. Better not drop in there; that would mean my doom.

I thought back to the moment my father told me about this journey. I remembered how enthusiastic I was only a day ago, eager to prove myself on the battlefield, to gain honour and glory for my family. I surveyed the crew gathered around Jan, each a seasoned warrior. Then I glanced at the cog we had tracked since dawn. It was Flemish, the men said, all eyes gazing at our prize.

Our objective was to capture such vessels and take their belongings. Jan explained this was called privateering, a sanctioned way of seizing goods from any ship that refused to pay taxes at the harbour. The captain would give half of what we took to the castellan, dividing the rest among the crew. And so, as luck would have it, we had spent the better part of the morning tracking this Flemish merchant cog, now closing in fast.

Despite my lack of combat experience, I knew this was a momentous opportunity to prove myself. I listened intently as Jan outlined the plan, his gruff voice ringing over the choppy waves.

'They carry wool and possibly silver,' Jan assessed. He saw profit.

'Easy pickings,' Trollmann judged, his stare calm, emotionless. 'Looks like easy pickings,' he declared. 'But watch out men. They seem to be building them taller these days. It won't be a small jump.'

He turned his gaze to me, his tone dry. 'Sure you're up for it, lass? With your iron dress?' The crew erupted into laughter, their eyes twinkling. All of them were dressed in leather tabards or padded gambesons, their attire practical and functional.

I gritted my teeth, refusing to let their mockery get the best of me. Still a novice in combat, I was determined to prove my worth. Steeling myself, I stepped forward to join the rest of the crew, my eyes fixed on the prize ahead.

'Normally,' Jan agreed, 'I would also wear mail protection, lad, but these cogs are like the face of a mountain; you have to climb their straight wooden walls and armour is too heavy. Besides, they have maybe fifteen armed men on that vessel, and none of them are true fighters. We can easily best them.'

As I glanced back, I saw Frethirik nodding vigorously at his father's words, a grin on his face. Damn him, I thought to myself. I would show him what I was made of soon enough.

Reluctantly, I frowned, avoiding the looks from the rest of the crew. Despite my nerves, I just wanted to wear my armour into battle. I felt safer that way.

Our ship surged forward, cutting through the waves towards the Flemish cog, the men holding our grappling hooks. The plan was simple: board the cog as soon as we got close enough and slay everyone standing in our way. As we approached the Flemish cog, my heart began to race. This was my first battle, and I imagined myself standing tall and proud, a sword in one hand and a shield in the other, facing the Flemish warriors with honour.

My hands trembled as thoughts of victory rushed through my body. I pictured myself moving with deadly precision, my sword cutting through the air as I took down my opponents one by one. In my mind's eye, I saw the Flemish crew cowering before me, their weapons no match for my skill and bravery.

I watched the expressions of the Flemish merchants. Their eyes widened with fear, some anxiously guarding their goods while others pled for mercy, knowing our approach was imminent. Two children, barely of age to work on the ship, wailed uncontrollably, filling the air with a mix of sweat, brine, and hysteria.

My nerves ran higher as we neared the cog's side. I had longed for my first battle for so long, and even though the Flemish merchants looked nothing like the fierce warriors from the stories, I couldn't wait to finally prove myself in combat. I desperately wanted to return home to Father, boasting how I had killed some Flemish, looting their silver. The thought of it filled me with pride and excitement.

Our snekkja finally reached the side of the high cog. Jan raised his hand, ordering us to wait for his signal, but in my youthful excitement, I disregarded his strict command. Without thinking, I leaped forward to be the first to board the enemy ship. Or at least, that's what I intended.

With a fierce war cry on my lips, I jumped onto the high wooden wall of the enemy's vessel, gripping the rope ladder tightly as I pulled myself up. The thrill of the moment gave me the strength to haul myself up and onto the enemy ship despite the weight of my hauberk. But just as I reached the top, something hit me hard, and I struggled to maintain my balance. My fingers frantically grasped the rope ladder as I tried to keep from falling. My arms ached with exertion, and terror seized my heart. Looking down into the darkness, I imagined the black, murky depths of the bogs back home, and I fought hard not to panic.

Then my grip slipped.

My heart pounded as I braced for impact, falling headfirst through the biting wind into the watery darkness.

I awoke to voices, yet I couldn't see anything, a pitch-black haze obscuring my vision. Suddenly, I heard my mother singing. Where was I? Was I in bed? Why couldn't I wake up? I reached out to feel for my nightshirt, water dropping on my head. Seriously, again? Had no one repaired the roof yet?

Feeling a splash on my face, I gasped for air. The haze before my eyes slowly lifted. Trollmann's face came into focus, muttering, 'Ah, he's fine, Frethirik. He probably has a headache, though.'

Frethirik now entered my view, helping me sit up. He explained that after Jan pulled me from the water, I remained unconscious while the rest of the men boarded the cog, easily climbing over its high walls without the burden of metal rings on their bodies.

'It was so glorious, Reginhard! I killed a bastard straight away,' Frethirik shouted in my ear. I slapped him away, my head cracking like a nut. It hurt so much, and the fact that Frethirik was now a warrior while I was still a whimpering lass was almost too much to bear.

'Trollmann was savage too, mate!' He just went on as if he hadn't noticed my sour-faced reaction. Or perhaps he didn't care. 'He went overboard with his two seaxes. It was all intestines and blood the moment he set foot on the cog.'

'You just had to wait a bit longer, lass.' Trollmann's know-it-all face reappeared. 'And I told you not to wear that vest.'

As Trollmann chided me, I noticed some of the rings on my arm sleeve were bent slightly. I winced at the bruise. 'How did this happen?' I asked.

'Well,' Trollmann replied. 'You were a bit right wearing your vest, lad. One of the Flemish on the high prow hurled a harpoon at you. You dropped straight over the side again.'

Jan neared us, clapping me hard on the back. 'Luckily for you, the fisherman's tool was as blunt as a hammer.'

By now, our men had successfully taken control of the cog, unloading its riches, including five and ten sacks of high-quality wool, a large pile of silver, and various coins found on the merchants. Our men worked quickly and efficiently, with the giant Rurik taking inventory of all the goods to divide them among the crew.

The two Flemish children were taken as prisoners, while the rest were killed in the fight. Rurik interrogated the youngsters about the ship's trade routes, destinations, and any other valuable information that could lead us to other Flemish cogs. Then, their ship was stripped of its tools, weapons, and the crew's belongings, while the captured goods and the prisoners would be taken back.

'We'll release them once we're back in Thuredrith,' Jan grunted. 'Next time, wait until our ship is aligned with theirs.' He smiled, pointing at the lower area of the cog, 'and then jump onto that part.' A wave of embarrassment washed over me. Oh, how foolish I had been! All I needed to do was exercise a bit of patience before jumping; my eagerness to prove my worth had completely overtaken me.

'At least you learned humility, right lad?' Jan murmured, his deep voice rumbling with laughter. The crew met his words with a chorus of hearty chuckling, everyone finding humour in my near death. I couldn't help but join them, although it tasted as sour as a plum.

'Come on, you'll be all right,' Trollmann clasped me on the back, trying to reassure me. 'You are, after all, a true warrior, right?' He flashed another grin. 'Well, almost.'

Chapter Four

The next few days, the sea seemed empty of traders. No matter how hard we tried, we found no other ships, so Jan decided to head back. As was customary, we divided the spoils amongst the crew, with one sack set aside to be given to my father as compensation for taking care of Frethirik.

As we sailed closer to the harbour of Thuredrith, Jan motioned for us to come to him, chewing on a piece of salty fish. 'I have something important to discuss with you both,' he announced.

I quickly brushed some bread crumbs off my cheek, eager to hear what he had to say. 'What is it, father?' Frethirik asked, spitting out some fish scales into the sea.

Jan turned to his son first. 'Frethirik, it's about time you took on more responsibilities. You can't rely on Reginhard's father to take care of you forever, so I would like you to join the crew.' Jan then glanced at me. 'It is a good thing that Salaco taught you to fight, especially on horseback, although I heard you were not great at it.'

Frethirik raised his brows. 'I prefer steering boats anyway.'

'Well, I still think it's good that you've seen what it's like on an estate,' Jan said, looking down at us both. 'Perhaps one day you will have one of your own. Maybe both of you.'

'Help each other from now on,' Trollmann added. 'Because that's what will get you furthest in life. True brotherhood. Always stay loyal to each other.'

'Yeah and I am done having to share my spoils with your

father, who is getting richer every year!' Jan joked. 'How many sheep does he own by now? Twenty-five? He can produce his own wool. I no longer have to steal more for him.'

'That does sound like quite the brotherhood, the both of you,' I replied. I couldn't help but sound cynical. I was still annoyed and, frankly, quite jealous. Bloody Frethirik becoming a warrior before me.

In Thuredrith, Jan oversaw the loading of goods and then reported to the castellan. Frethirik and I headed to Veenkoop. My mood was as sour as a plum. I dreaded facing my father's disappointment, and I just couldn't believe Frethirik had killed while I lay on the planks of our ship. God, how my brother would laugh when he heard this.

As we trudged back, I also had to endure Frethirik's boasting all the way to Aitet's shed. But when we finally arrived, we suddenly spotted Gerold racing towards us. He stumbled out of some brown reeds, his hands drenched in blood, with a wet patch near his privates. He jumped up and down, unable to speak coherently.

'M-my lord,' he stuttered as tears flowed from frightened eyes. 'V-Veenkoop burns, and angry men with beards and swords are slaying everyone.' Frethirik and I glanced at each other with wide eyes. My heart pounded, my mouth suddenly dry. I managed to subdue an enormous desire to rush to Veenkoop at once.

My mind raced with thoughts. What could we do to help our village? I couldn't just stand by while homes burned and our people were slaughtered. Jan's words rang in my head: 'True brotherhood. Always stay loyal to each other.' I glanced toward Frethirik, his eyes still wide. We had to devise a plan to protect the people we loved.

I gently placed a hand on Gerold's shoulders. 'Calm down, boy. Now listen. Do you see the tree line up ahead? Run to these trees as fast as you can and hide, you hear me? Now go. Run to the forest.' I gestured wildly. 'Run. Run!' And run he did. He truly was the fastest runner I'd ever seen in my life, thank God.

I took a deep breath, trying to focus on the situation. Despite the worries for my family, I knew we had to act fast. 'Frethirik,' I said, turning to my friend. 'Go back to Thuredrith again. If they're not under attack too, then for God's sake, get anyone to help us. Get your father and the men over here. Please, go to them immediately!'

'But what about you Reginhard. Won't you join me?'

'Don't worry Frethirik. I'm just going to see what's happening, but I'll be careful.'

'All right then, I'll be back soon. Don't do anything before the crew gets here.' With a quick nod, Frethirik spurred his horse and galloped off. When he disappeared from sight, I turned towards Veenkoop, swallowing my fear.

Taking Winney by the harnesses, I moved towards the village's periphery. Tying off the reins, I crept through the reeds on the edge of Veenkoop, crawling through the mud until I could view the town through a thick patch of reeds.

It was like a knife piercing my heart. Tears welled as I saw my mother, Ome Aitet, and most of the farmers lying dead on the muddy ground, their improvised weapons still in their hands. 'Mother,' I whispered, unable to believe it. An unbearable pain gripped my chest. I couldn't breathe.

Suddenly, a blood-curdling scream pierced the scene as a massive warrior emerged from a hovel, dragging Gerda by the hair. His black beard was visible under a goggled helmet that shaded cold, dark eyes. The air froze around me. My heart pounded in my chest like a drumbeat of pure dread. Still, I couldn't tear my gaze away from the horror unfolding before me. A gasp caught in my throat, and my breath hitched as I watched in shock and disbelief.

'Behold, my mighty warriors,' he shouted in a heavy Danish accent, his voice booming across the village square. His fellow murderers cheered in response, waving their blood-splattered axes. He took two steps forward, raising his hand. 'We destroy the Frankish village. Let this be a message to all the followers of Wiltenburg!'

Pain and anger surged within. If this was an ordinary raid, I just couldn't comprehend the significance of Wiltenburg. What the hell was happening to us? Was this the kind of Viking attack grandfather had told us about? I thought they were a thing of the past.

The Viking continued, hate etched into every pore on his scarred face. 'Today, we end these stains on this earth. Today we end Salaco, the murderer of my father, Ivar One Eye.'

Dear God. This man was an old enemy of my father's then.

After a brief invocation to Odin, the Viking leader raised his sword. My stomach churned, and bile rose in my throat. The Viking's sword sliced open Gerda's chest, her breasts cut from her body. He then tossed her onto the ground, her agonizing sobs carrying in the wind. I covered my mouth, forcing myself not to scream. I felt helpless.

Suddenly, a deafening roar erupted from our hoeve. After a moment of bated silence, heavy hooves pounded the earth. My father, in full armour, emerged from the stable area. The sunlight glinted off his hauberk, making it shine like polished silver. His face twisted in anger. What could he do against so many? He surveyed the carnage, his veins bulging in his neck, his jaw tense. A mix of rage and anguish on his face was more than I could bear.

A hush fell over the scene. My father glanced at Mother's dead body before turning towards his enemy, his eyes shooting flames.

He must have been putting on his armour when the village got attacked, I thought, noticing his lack of mailed mittens. He had probably rushed back as quickly as he could, only to witness . . . only to see what lay before us – the destruction of everything we loved.

'Ragnar Ivarson,' he bellowed. 'Never did I expect to see you again, especially after we dismissed your longboat five years ago. At least your thieving goat of a father got what he deserved, as will you now.'

Sliding the sword from its scabbard, Father pointed it at the Viking leader. 'How dare you raid my estate, kill my wife, and slaughter my peasants! I'll make you pay, and I promise you shall never see Valhalla. You will burn in the fires of Hell!'

With a fierce battle cry, my father flung his sword, spurring his horse forward. The ground trembled under Roar's hooves as he charged towards the enemy, his mane flying wildly in the wind. With a deft maneuver, my father aimed his blade at the first Viking in his path. The man barely had time to react before my father's sword impaled him, skewering his body and lifting him off the ground. Blood spurted from the wound as the warrior fell to the ground, writhing in agony.

Yet Roar didn't slow, his momentum carrying my father forward to the next target. His face now a mask of pure rage, his eyes a blazing fury, he charged towards the next enemy. I watched in awe as he dispatched one Viking after another with brutal efficiency, his sword and shield working in tandem to inflict maximum damage, hacking, battering, slicing, and bashing.

As he fought, my father let out a primal roar as if channeling all his revenge into his blows. Never had I seen him like this, a terrifying sight, and I knew that the Vikings stood no chance one on one. But then, just as my father was about to deliver another blow, tragedy struck. Ragnar's axe connected with my father's horse, causing the destrier to stumble and fall, taking my father down with it.

I couldn't breathe; my father lay motionless on the ground. My heart dropped. At that moment, everything fell silent except for the pounding of my heart.

Trapped under the rump of his trusty steed, my father lay there helpless. Panic overtook my senses. My hand started shaking as I held my sword hilt, tightening my grip. What could I do? How could I help?

I wanted to rush into the fray, but I knew there was nothing I could do. I stood there frozen, paralyzed by my helplessness, my mind a complete blur. My mother lay lifeless before me, while my father, trapped under his horse, was now on the brink of death. I wanted to scream, cry, lash out, but could only stand there, my sword held limply at my side.

My chest heaved, anger filling every pore as I fought for control and heeded my father's training. One against so many was certain death. But how could I not? Frethirik, where are you? Where is the help we need? I watched in despair as my father groaned, his cheeks flushed, struggling in vain to free himself from the heavy beast.

Ragnar Ivarson stood silently, his eyes fixed on my father's struggle. He inhaled deeply, a grin spreading across his scarred visage. 'You see, Frank,' he sneered. 'Your kind is only good for raising livestock and clearing land.'

My father groaned as he tried to move.

'You just hide behind your baileys, Frank. Using your steeds instead of trusting your own muscle.' Ragnar's eyes widened. 'You even called yourself a Viking, while all you did was hide behind the brave men of Jan Ubbeson.' Ragnar's face now turned a deep red. 'My father died a true warrior, sword in hand, flying towards Valhalla with honour. And what of you, Frank? You will die like the coward you are, crushed under the hooves of your own horse.'

Ragnar Ivarson laughed as his face twisted into something demonic. 'And I want you to know that your filthy Frank head will forever adorn my warship, reminding all that Salaco of Veenkoop died by my hand,' he pointed his sword at my father. 'A warning that your kind will never beat us Norse at sea.'

Ragnar raised his blade, but my father fixed his eyes on him. 'Know this, Viking. You may kill me today, but it is your kind that has ultimately been beaten,' he declared, his voice strained with the weight of the horse on top of him.

My father spat out some blood. 'You may kill me today, but you well know that our mottes and baileys have kept you out since my generation. So while you raid our villages with your handful of pitiful warriors, you will never defeat our bishop's disciplined army. Soon the Thuredrith men will arrive, and their Frankish horsemen will be your downfall.'

The Viking warriors flicked their eyes east, their voices growing quieter. They started to murmur among themselves, their brows furrowing. I smiled in smug satisfaction. Fear. Father had chinked their armour, as they sensed their days of easy raiding were ending.

In a sudden and noble act, my father's hand darted towards his belt, seizing the hilt of his knife. Before I could even comprehend his intention, he drew the blade across his own throat in a swift and violent motion. Blood gushed out, staining his armour and the ground beneath him. Shock and grief slammed into me, and tears flowed unabated. I clamped a hand over my mouth, holding back my anguish.

As I watched my father take his last breath, I couldn't help but admire his sacrifice. Frisian pride swelled inside me. He'd snatched away Ragnar's revenge with one swipe of a blade. By sacrificing his life, Father had taken the devil's victory. Yet, he would be welcomed into God's arms this day, death valiant and brave, no matter what the priest claimed about suicide resulting in purgatory.

Though my life would never be the same, the memory of my parents' lifeless bodies lying in the blood-soaked peat and my immense pride in Father's noble sacrifice will forever burn in my heart. My earthly father, protector, and guide was gone. Yet, he lives, flying into the welcoming arms of angels.

A cloud of destruction hung over the burning village as our hoeve was devoured by fire and smoke. The seafarers pillaged what was left of my home, slaughtering the few remaining villagers.

As the flames consumed everything I held dear, my chest was gripped by panic and confusion. I sat trapped in grief until a pale face appeared from the reeds, staring down at me. It took me a moment to realise this was a Viking, now opening his mouth. 'Intruder, intruder!'

Before his mates responded to his alert, I unsheathed my sword, channeling all my rage and sorrow into my weapon. I raised my shield in a defensive pose and charged forward, fast but under control. My father's training would see me through now.

Yet the warrior had enough time to react. He swung his axe as I bashed into him, trying to hammer the weapon into my body. I swerved to the right and repeatedly slashed my blade against my enemy's shield, probing for weakness.

It didn't take long before I saw an opening. I jabbed my opponent, luring him into attacking me again, only to step back when he charged. I dodged, swerving to the right, where he tripped over some reeds and dropped to the ground. Wasting no time, I hammered him on the head with the sword, ramming all my anger onto his helmet until it was pulp. Leaving him to rot, I raced to Winney as footsteps and shouts closed in.

I hunched over my horse, evading the arrows they loosed. I subdued all my inner pain and focused all my energy on reaching Thuredrith. My Father was right. Revenge was coming. Our horsemen would charge down upon them, leaving no one alive.

Chapter Five

As I thundered past Ome Aitet's hut, perched on the terp, memories of the old overseer flooded my mind. I closed my eyes, stung by the picture of Ome Aitet lying in a pool of blood. Then, something suddenly caught my attention on the river. Squinting, I spotted Gerold ferrying the gamekeeper's trusty raft across the river. I crossed myself, mumbling a quick prayer for his safe escape.

Yet when Gerold made his way onto the riverbed, heading north into the peatlands, I couldn't help but worry he might get trapped in the marches. I shouted, trying to warn him, but he didn't even stop once. I kept calling until I reached the woods between Veenkoop and Thuredrith, where I eventually lost sight of him.

With a heavy heart, I told myself, 'well, at least one villager managed to escape safely.' It felt like a small glimmer of hope amidst the chaos, but it was at least something to hold onto. I rode on, my mind swirling with doubts.

As Thuredrith appeared on the horizon, I wondered if I had truly escaped the raiders. I peered behind me. The dirt road was deserted, but I knew I couldn't let my guard down just yet. They could emerge from the woods at any moment.

As I halted, I had to dismount, feeling sick. Retching, I almost choked as I threw up in the grass. My beloved mother, who had always provided comfort during challenging times, and my father, who had taught me everything I knew, were both gone. The innocent villagers who worked tirelessly to provide for their families. And Gerda. Sweet, beautiful, Gerda. All dead.

Blinking, I took a deep breath as I fought back tears that threatened to spill, and tried to focus. What could I do? Focus Reginhard. Though I felt cold and empty inside, I knew I had to move on. Had to get to Thuredrith. Maybe Jan was still there. And where was Frethirik? In town already, fetching help?

Then, it hit me like a bolt of lightning. My brother was still in town. How could I forget? If anyone could help me now, it was him. Gritting my teeth, I mounted Winney and spurred her forward, hope igniting within me. Maybe, just maybe, there was still a chance for us.

I rode on until the sight of Thuredrith's wooden palisade slowly appeared in the distance. The wind swept across the vast, open field, the river Thure flowing on my left, wild and untamed. Despite the prospect of finding my brother, I remained numbed by what I had just survived. As I approached the town, it seemed to tower over me like a giant guardian, standing watch over the surrounding landscape. 'It didn't guard Veenkoop, though,' I whispered, unease growing within my gut. Something felt wrong about all this.

A movement caught my eye in the distance. As I strained to see better, I recognised the shapes of men in a circle, discussing something among themselves. They were about a quarter mile from the town's gates, and I couldn't quite make out who they were. Squinting, I tried to get a better look, unsure whether they were friendly.

'Well, we'll just have to find out Winney. They're not on horseback, so let's just go for it.' I decided I could still escape on Winney's back if they proved hostile.

Getting closer, I noticed that all wore mail shirts or leather tabards, but I couldn't quite place them. I kept moving forward, keeping a close eye on their reactions. Nearing them within a hundred feet, one of their men broke away from the group. My heart raced, shoulders tense. I grabbed my reins, ready to flee, but then the man held up his hands.

'Reginhard, it's me.' It wasn't until he took off his helmet that I was sure. I almost couldn't believe my eyes, jumping from Winney's back. It was Frethirik, accompanied by Trollmann and about half the crew. Finally, help had arrived.

Yet when they came into view, their downcast faces plunged me into doubt again. Something was wrong. Frethirik rushed forward to meet me, his flushed face sweaty and red. 'Reginhard, there you are! Bad news, I'm afraid. The castellan's refusing to help.' He paused, taking a breath. 'I found my father who told me everything was in lockdown. After hearing what happened at Veenkoop, he commanded me and Trollmann, with half of the men, to look for you on foot while he prepares to sail away from the harbour.'

'What!' I couldn't believe it. 'Why on earth would the castellan order a lockdown? He needs to help us!'

'I fear foul play lad.' Trollmann answered, his frown darker than ever before. 'But look, Jan now readies our ship to sail towards your father's estate. We will do all we can to help.'

Trollmann's eyes widened. 'Dear God lad. What happened to you? You look as pale as a full moon in the northern lights. What happened in Veenkoop?'

I couldn't keep my eyes from staring at the ground below, unable to face anyone. 'Trollmann, it is too late. My parents . . . .' My voice trailed off as I broke down completely, falling to my knees, the weight of everything that had happened just too much to bear.

I spilled out my grief for several moments until I felt the comforting touch of Trollmann's hand on my shoulder. I shook my head, wiping the tears from my face. I knew I couldn't cry and lose control now. I had to do something. Anger returned at the memory of Ragnar slaying my father. I knew I had to fight; I wanted to kill all these Viking bastards, but at the same time, I still felt so helpless. Hell, what could we do to them with just a dozen men? They must have numbered at least forty.

Frethirik gently offered me a sack of ale. After taking a few sips, my nerves began to calm, the liquid comforting my dry throat. Recovered enough to speak coherently, I told the men everything that happened in the village.

Trollmann listened attentively, nodding after I finished. 'Look, we have to move Reginhard. We will avenge your family. Every last drop of the scourge will be spilt. This I swear. But first, we march to Veenkoop, and carefully scout the place. Maybe some villagers yet live and we can help those escape.'

As I regained some semblance of control, I considered what we could do against these Vikings. And then it hit me; tactics. My father had always taught me tactics were the key to winning battles.

I faced Frethirik, feeling a new light emerge from the shadows of my mind. 'How do long you reckon until your father sails past us?' I glanced at the river, considering the ship's speed.

My friend, his face still filled with tears, now frowned. 'Damn, yeah. My father . . . he will sail past the town soon Reginhard. We should see him appear on the Thure passing the town at any moment now, I guess. Can't be long.'

I gazed at Thuredrith, a settlement surrounded by the river as if God had placed it within a horseshoe. So Jan's ship should appear from the left side of the town then.

As I focused my thoughts, a vision formed. A memory that

was so tangible and real I could almost touch it. I heard my father speak to me as if he was actually there. 'Remain calm, Reginhard. Even if an entire conroi of your men get slaughtered in front of you. Always make tactical decisions. Even when your mates die around you, you can still save others. Grieving is to be done later. To defeat your enemies on the battlefield, remain focused.'

I nodded, resolved now to finish this business once and for all. We'll kill these Vikings for you, Father. I turned to Trollmann. 'Take the men to the edge of the village, near Aitet's place.'

The hut was located on the terp, making it an excellent defensive position for infantry. It lay higher than the surrounding flat fields, and any defenders lining up there had the advantage of the rivers on both sides, which prevented attackers from flanking them.

'Trollmann, with God's help, I just saw Gerold escape on Aitet's small ferry, so the raft is now on our side of the river. You can use it to get to the hut.'

'Ah, I see, Reginhard. That's the place to take them on then,' the Sami replied with a nod.

'Indeed,' I said. 'And while you take the ferry to Aitet's hut, I will wait here for Jan so I can board his ship when he sails past the town. I can direct him to you, so we can crush the Vikings from two sides.'

He nodded at me before turning around again. 'All right,' he said. 'But I just hope you get there soon though, because otherwise, we could get trapped at that hut. And with their numbers, they'll kill us on the spot.'

'I know, but don't worry,' I replied, my confidence returning. 'Me and Jan should be there soon and then we have the advantage of surprise. If you stand firm at the terp, you can hold the Vikings until we get to you. It is a great defensive position, allowing you to keep them checked until we enclose them from two sides.' I battered my fists together. 'Then we kill every last of them bastards.'

Trollmann grinned now, swirling around to face the crew. 'All right men, you heard Reginhard. It is a fine plan. Let's kill Ragnar's bastards then. You can keep any silver you loot from their dead bodies!'

The warriors roared 'Death to Ragnar,' then rushed en masse towards Veenkoop, leaving me to wait for Jan. I waved them goodbye, knowing that with only a few miles to cover, they would get there soon.

Chapter Six

I decided to wait for Jan at the riverside. But just as I turned to move, an arrow thudded into the ground ten feet away from me, jolting me into caution. I immediately raised my shield, facing the town, where two figures now towered over the gateway.

'You will go no further, you little bastard,' a rumbling voice carried in the wind, barely audible from this distance. I paused. Where did it come from, and who could this be?

A slender man in full armour, its surcoat displaying a red lion, appeared on Thuredrith's ramparts. A nasal helmet covered most of his thin face, a thick black beard protruding from underneath. The wind picked up, tugging at the sleeves of my gambeson. I squinted. Who could this be? He had to be someone of importance to address me from Thuredrith's walls.

He pointed at me. 'You, pup. The castellan tells me you're Salaco's son.'

Another figure sprung up next to the mysterious man. To my surprise, he held up a shield displaying that same red lion, certainly not a vassal of Wiltenburg's bishop, our liege.

Where had I seen that coat of arms before? Going through all the crests I knew, I scrutinised every detail until it suddenly dawned on me – a red lion. My father told stories of how he shot Count Dirk of Holland just before his standard bearer dropped the banner, a red lion on a gold background. But that couldn't be right. Thuredrith was in the service of our bishop, so what was the castellan doing? What in God's name was happening?

The lean figure addressed me again, scowling under the iron helmet. 'Know that I am the count of Holland, the rightful liege of Thuredrith,' he bellowed.

Clasping my hand over my mouth, I tried to process who stood before me. It simply couldn't be true – Count Floris, the brother of the man my father had killed. This archenemy of our bishop must somehow have claimed Thuredrith, convincing its castellan into his service.

Alone on this windy grassy field, there was no one to turn to for support. The gravity of the situation was sinking in, and I had to act. A sharp despair rose in my chest as I eyed the gates. Somehow, I still managed to find my voice.

'My lord count. I only know that Veenkoop is my father's estate, and is under attack. Sea raiders just killed my entire family.'

While I couldn't believe I told this to a man supposed to be our enemy, I had to convey the urgency of the situation. In all logic, he wouldn't want any raiders near the town either, for his own sake.

'Please open the gates and lend me assistance.'

Count Floris glared, hammering the wooden rampart in front of him. 'Yeah? Why would I assist the man who killed my brother and then colonised my land without any right?'

I seethed with rage as the pieces came together. It made sense. The killing of my family, Veenkoop in flames – all of it orchestrated by Count Floris. He sent Ragnar and his Viking band to destroy our village. He wanted it all for himself.

Clutching the hilt of my sword, I stared up at him. This was the true villain; the one who had masterminded all that death, killing everyone I cherished with his vendetta. Unsheathing my sword, I roared at the source of my misery – I would never forget this – never forgive him. Crossing myself, I swore to slaughter Count Floris one day.

The count smirked down at me, waving his hand. 'And now you follow him to the grave pup!'

The heavy wooden gates flew open, and six armoured horsemen stormed out.

'Damn,' I muttered. What could I do? How could I escape from this? I couldn't fight six seasoned warriors. Maybe the woods behind me? But that was back to Veenkoop, and I would still need to outride them.

They thundered out of the wooden gate like demons, lances pointing forward. Their nasal helmets gave them a ghost-like appearance, all emotion hidden beneath the iron protection. Lining up as one, they pounded the earth in a rhythm of death, roaring.

With the threat of dying over me, I glanced at the river. Just about to lose all hope, my eyes caught sight of Jan's ship passing town. Crossing myself, I beamed with relief, laughing out loud like a madman.

A make-or-break moment. If I could just reach that ship, I could haul myself and Winney on board and escape from the clutches of the riders. Focus, I thought. The enemy horsemen were faster, and my horse was growing tired. But they were still a quarter mile away, my only chance. I kicked the stirrups, rushing Winney forward as quickly as she could carry me.

After riding a few hundred feet, I glanced behind me. Floris' men neared me. I shook the reins again. Trampling the grass and bushes beneath her hooves, Winney did what she could, but we still had halfway to go before we reached Jan.

One of the riders rode faster than the others and approached me from my right, pointing his lance at my back. Clad in a leather tabard, he roared, 'I'll spear you, little bastard. For the Count.'

Instinctively, I threw down my lance, holding my shield ready in my left hand. Now in range, the warrior lunged at me, forcing me to dodge his blow as I moved to the left. I felt the lance slide past my hauberk, but no pain. Now, I thought, as I grabbed the lance before it slipped past me, pulling as hard as I could.

The warrior lost his balance, the momentum of his charge lunging him forward. He clung to the reins, trying to regain his footing, but it was too late. Hurtling through the air, he crashed to the ground, his shield breaking, his helmet clanging against a rock.

Yet the other riders were approaching, their roars growing louder. I focused on the ship, envisioning Jan's men pointing their crossbows. The captain paced across the deck, shouting commands at his men. I caught a faint, 'Wait for it.'

I glanced behind me again. The five remaining horsemen thundered on, and I knew it would be a close call. I couldn't take on five lances, so I braced myself for the inevitable. My right hand went to the silver cross around my neck. This was the end. Nothing I could do to stop it.

As I closed my eyes, visions of my family flooded my mind. Ome Aitet put a reassuring hand on Gerold's shoulder, smiling at me and my brother from a distance. My mother waved at us from the doorway of our Hoeve, a basket of fruit in her hands. The apples shone like gold in the sunlight. My mouth felt dry, and I turned to move to the hoeve. 'Always watch out for trickery, Reginhard.' My father suddenly tripped me onto the floor of the training ground as my family disappeared into the dark.

The shouts returned, bringing me back to reality. I could hear the sound of hooves pounding the ground and a rush of air as a lance flew by my shoulder, just an inch away. I kicked Winney one last time, knowing that death closed in. I lifted my gaze to the heavens, accepting my fate. Maybe it was better this way. Maybe God wanted me to be with my family. 'Embrace me, oh Lord.'

Suddenly, a piercing whistle sounded, followed by a barrage of bolts flying past me. They crashed into my assailers, taking down two horsemen at once. The bolts penetrated their armour with sickening thuds, and the riders slipped from their horses and crashed into the ground. And just as I had given up, a wave of bolts struck down the assailants.

The remaining horsemen frantically looked around and, pointing at the ship, shouted warnings. They swirled around their horses, turning back to town. And just like that, I was in front of the ship – winded, sweaty, clutching my silver cross – but alive.

Jan's snekkja gracefully glided up onto the bank of the river. The sun broke through the clouds as the ship slid into the soft mud. The crew stood ready to receive me, helping me load Winney onto the boat. Overwhelmed with gratitude, I shook the men's hands, knowing how narrowly I had escaped death.

Aboard ship, Jan, donned in his full armour, came to greet me. He embraced me like a father would his child, his face flushed, his eyes burning with intensity. It was clear he was ready to unleash hell. 'Damn it lad!' he exclaimed. 'That bloody count just walked up to me and told me to forget our deal with the castellan. I even had to hand him all the silver we plundered.'

He glanced down momentarily, gathering his thoughts before facing me again. 'Your brother . . . ,' he started, but the words stuck in his throat. 'I'm sorry, lad. We've been betrayed. The count just captured him.' His tone softened, his blue eyes turning wet. 'How is your father? Do you know where he is?'

Jan's words hit me like a hammer, the day's reality slamming into me. A sharp pain in my chest left me speechless as I struggled to gather my thoughts. Finally, I shook my head, trying to find my voice. 'Ragnar . . . killed them,' I managed, my mind still reeling from shock.

As soon as the words left my mouth, Jan understood the gravity of the situation. The look in his eyes told me he knew what had happened to his friend and my family. Tears welled in his eyes as he bellowed that he would crush Ragnar to death for what he had done.

Strangely, Jan's intense rage gave me a glimmer of hope and a sudden surge of courage. Seeing him so fiercely motivated to take down Ragnar and his followers made me realise I didn't stand alone in my desire for revenge. My father had been his best friend, his vrindr, his companion in war and life. The thought of killing them all, every last one of those bastards, fueled me with burning. It was time to act.

But then, as I glanced back at the town walls, my blood ran cold. Count Floris roared at us, and I could barely make out the word 'brother.' Then, a smile crossed his lips as he flung a severed head over the walls with the same casualness one might toss a bone to a dog.

My brother's death hit me like a sledgehammer, knocking me down to the deck. My chest tightened, my heart shattering, tears streaming down my face. My brother, my only remaining family member . . . gone too, just like that.

Chapter Seven

I let out a gut-wrenching scream to the heavens, my voice trembling. Jan, wincing beside me, placed a hand on my shoulder, unable to find the words to ease my pain. The unbearable ache in my heart made it impossible to come to terms with all that had happened that day.

I breathed in and out, in and out, closing my eyes, the cool air rushing in and out of my lungs. I saw my brother's face, his warm smile. I heard his infectious laughter, his coarse jokes. We had grown up together in Veenkoop, always by each other's side. We trained together, raced together, jousted together. He was always there for me, and now he was gone too. Why was our world so full of hate? Why did we have to kill each other's families like this? Had my father ever expected all this to come out of his victory over Holland?

I clutched the cross again. Amidst this agony, somehow, I held on to a shred of faith. Focus Reginhard. Maybe the Vikings hadn't killed everyone. Who knows who could have escaped? And if they did survive, we had to help them.

Jan remained silent, his arm draped around me. I sat down and began to explain everything, starting with the brutal murder of my family. Words spilled out as I described the standoff between my father and Ragnar. Jan just listened, hanging on to every word.

After finishing my tale, recounting Trollmann's march towards Aitet's hut, I sighed deeply. The fate of so many rested on the outcome of the battle. I watched Jan, aware that our lives still hung in the balance. 'Jan, if we're quick, we can damage Ragnar's ship while he attacks Trollmann and Frethirik. Then we attack him from behind.' I bashed my fists together. 'Like that.'

Jan raised his brows. His smile returned, but it was small and tinged with sadness. Despite his attempts to hide it, a frown remained etched on his face. His hand moved to his chin, and then he nodded in approval. 'It's a simple and straightforward plan, lad, and I think it can work. You're a bold strategist, aren't you? Just like your father.'

Jan then grabbed my shoulders, his eyes beaming again. 'Since Trollmann will form a line at Aitet's hut, we could take the crossbows and try to sneak up behind Ragnar's men. The terp will hide our ship's approach. First, we shoot them in the back, and then we charge them.'

His brief optimism quickly turned back into a grimace of pain, the blue of his eyes darkening like the deep ocean. 'Look, I am so sorry about your family Reginhard. So often I have seen it in life. War is always full of horror, a far cry from the glory many lords pretend it to be, but this time, now it is personal. Know that I feel your pain too.' He looked down, clearly fighting the upcoming tears. 'My brother in arms, oh God . . . .'

His face reddened. 'The way of betrayal,' he spat, his voice sharp. 'That damn Ragnar again. I can't believe I'm even surprised that he's involved with that treacherous count.'

Jan then looked up to face his men, staring intensely into the eyes of each of them. His voice, firm and steady, addressed them with purpose. 'You heard the lad, men,' Jan declared. 'Our enemies have taken the life of my best friend and his kin. His villagers lay dead. His home is in ruins. My own base destroyed by the bloody hand of Ragnar.' He paused, his eyes scanning the faces of his men, his brows furrowed.

'But we will not stand idly by as they wreak such havoc. Let's put a stop to their senseless acts, avenge our brothers, and restore justice to my fallen comrade and his son. Make them pay for their crimes in blood.'

He raised his axe like Thor's hammer, his roar thundering over the river. This became a fight for survival, honour, and above all, vengeance. I felt confident we would not back down, Jan's warriors ready to help me avenge my family.

The warriors grumbled, throwing their weapons in the air. 'Cowards,' one greybeard murmured, 'I won't forget how they ran from us when Salaco cut down Ragnar's father. They're foul scum and will die like rodents under our blades.'

'Just right Ulfur!' Jan roared, facing Veenkoop's direction. 'God knows honour yet prevails amongst our side. Let us avenge our fallen brethren then. Let's send Ragnar and his heathens to Hell!'

After this mighty encouragement, the men rowed hard, our lean ship moving faster and faster on the deep river Thure, the men chanting an ancient song of revenge. The vessel turned into its own weapon, seething with hatred, our battle cries booming towards the heavens.

We sailed past Veenkoop's westernmost field, delighted to discover the enemy's boat there. Even better, the only souls within it were three boys no older than twelve, all asleep, each holding a mug half-full of ale.

'They didn't expect anyone to come from the water then?' I inquired.

Jan grunted. 'It is the comfort of betrayal, Reginhard. Still, only a poor captain doesn't weigh the possibility of unexpected circumstances.' Our captain's grin was almost back on his face.

Because the unexpected circumstances were twenty men armed with crossbows, axes, and swords. And we came for bloodshed.

We jumped ashore next to the Viking longship, knocking the boys out in case the drink hadn't been enough. A sack around their heads finished the job, after which their ship was ours.

'I liked your plan, lad, but we're changing it slightly,' Jan said after all the men had disembarked. 'I want five men here and fifteen to follow us with crossbows. The five guards will stay with our own ship. This way, we can still escape if things turn sour.'

He pointed at Ragnar's ship. 'We wouldn't want the same happening to us right?'

We all nodded as one. I wanted to kill as many of them as possible, a deep fury boiling in my stomach, just waiting to erupt.

Jan handed me a torch, the first token of my payback. After the men threw oil into Ragnar's snekkja, I put it to flame, the fire quickly engulfing the ship. The men cheered as the wooden planks crackled and snapped, the heat intense on my skin. The ship that had caused so much destruction and terror was steadily reduced to ash and rubble. Now, it was our turn.

Chapter Eight

After their ship was beyond salvation, we grabbed our crossbows and raced towards Aitet's hut, hiding behind the dykes. As we approached, we spotted Trollmann's smaller band of men, with their backs to the river, forming a defense against Ragnar and his Vikings.

The battle was bloody, ferocious. Despite their offensive, the Vikings couldn't flank Trollmann's war band. His warriors stood steadfast in the fork of the river, the terp's height of great help, as they pushed the Vikings back with their spears.

'Let's go then,' Jan shouted. 'Let's teach the bastards a lesson.'

We bellowed, 'For God and the fallen!' as we charged across the field, our crossbows ready to shoot at Jan's command. The captain held up his hand as we lined up in range. Then he signaled to fire. 'Unleash death!'

I heard a sickening thud of bolts striking their targets, followed by the screams of the wounded. One man went down gurgling, blood pouring out of his neck. Another fell backwards, struck in the chest, his body slamming into the ground. Our bolts confused their entire rank, their line turning into a bundle of blood and chaos.

Ragnar Ivarson swirled around, his face as white as a ghost. 'Cowards,' he hollered. Wasting no time, he restored order immediately, personally turning some of his warriors around, now rushing towards us.

That was it then, I thought. I crossed myself and watched the charging warriors in what felt like an eternity. I hadn't even taken my horse from the ship.

I shook off the doubt, hate overcoming my insecurity. It didn't matter whether I lived or died. I just wanted to hammer them. Hack some heads off. Just slay them, kill them all.

'Calm, my men,' Jan's steady voice commanded. 'Form up neatly and let them come at us. We break them with order in our ranks!'

We all knew what to do, training our entire lives for this moment. We lined up immediately, slinging the shields from our backs to unsheathe swords and axes. I put my kite shield in front of me, stepping slightly to the right, where the next man stood, our shields linking in an almost automatic rhythm. Training would soon be put to use.

As we waited for the enemy's approach, my heart pounded hard. I felt sweat drip from my face under my helmet, my knees shaking. A blond-haired warrior now charged towards me, his face obscured only by his helmet. His battle cry filled my ears as he closed in, his studded leather armour glinting in the sunlight.

As he drew closer, his eyes betrayed a flicker of fear. Then it struck me. I had seen him before. I suddenly remembered how he killed a child right in front of me. Boiling rage overwhelmed all else. I wanted nothing other than to slay this animal.

'Come on then,' I taunted, bashing my blade on my shield. 'Fly into my embrace.'

The moment took forever, like a dream. When he closed in, all the events of the day, the tension and fear, just faded away, a strange calm enveloping me. Usually so familiar, the grassy plains of my father's demesne now felt like a foreign and surreal landscape. Time slowed, my body bracing for impact.

As their warriors approached, it was clear that Ragnar had not thought his attack through. The Viking charge was undisciplined, with some warriors dashing far ahead of their comrades, spreading their forces thin across the battlefield.

I grinned at the opportunity. Gritting my teeth, my shield in front of me, they crashed into our line. We held our ground, not budging an inch, and when I looked up, I realized that my opponent was hardly older than me, his eyes wide as he screamed out words I didn't understand. He furiously hacked into my shield, but with each blow, his shield lowered. His mistake, I thought. I simply hacked my blade into him, slashing him with the sharp end of my sword, opening up his face into a pool of blood. He dropped onto his knees, twitching violently as he squirmed in misery. While his iron helmet protected his head, the front of his face was bashed in, with one eye completely pulverized. As he fell on the floor screaming, I stabbed him in his other eye, feeling the soft touch of his brain and the hard wall of his skull. That did him.

Another roar sounded. The next warrior lunged at me, so I had to put all thoughts of my kill aside. He swung his axe wildly, each blow crashing against my shield, splintering the wood and sending shards flying. The force of the impact shuddered through my arm, sweat pouring down my face. I gritted my teeth, resolved to survive this onslaught. I knew one slip up, one moment of hesitation, could mean my death.

But before I knew it, the warrior beside me finished my assailer with a single stroke of a heavy axe, shattering his leather helmet. Making a guttural sound, he twitched three times, dying on the spot.

And that was it; their charge stopped as soon as it started. At least ten enemy bodies lay dead at our feet, while three of ours had fallen. Across our line, we had clubbed and hammered the raiders into submission, their remainder now fleeing the scene. I cried out my victory at the clouds, hoping God saw me that day and saw how I fought rather than ran.

As the last Viking fell, we let out another deafening battle cry, our voices filled with the euphoria of victory. Some of our men broke formation, but Jan halted them with a sharp command. He called out to Trollmann, still on the other side of the field with the rest of the men. The Sami commander waved his two seaxes in response, signaling that their line also held.

Ragnar had no choice but to retreat, pulling back to the east, the only avenue of escape available, where they ran straight to the bridge leading into the woods.

Jan surveyed the battlefield, his eyes scanning until they suddenly widened. He whispered some calculations, then shouted a warning to Trollmann on the other side of the field. Pointing east, Jan bellowed across the meadows, 'Trollmann, get your men over here right now. We form one line and retreat.'

As Trollmann eyed the battlefield, his vision locking onto the east, he jumped up in alarm. Without hesitation, he began sprinting towards us, his men following suit.

Jan's experienced insight protected us from disaster. While Ivarson's panicked attack had failed, the war leader recovered quickly, turning his men towards the only direction left. He retreated eastward, preventing us from attacking him from two sides. But, as he did this, I missed one crucial element our captain had not.

Another enemy force approached us, led by the count and his men, numbering over fifty. The count stood at the forefront, mounted on horseback with a detachment of fifteen riders. His infantry lined up behind them, baying for blood. Ragnar and his remaining warriors scrambled to Count Floris, the Viking leader frantically shouting, pointing in our direction.

As I assessed the enemy, their armour and disciplined line impressed me. I knew the count's warriors could not be underestimated, appearing ruthless and skilled, their reputation preceding them. It was simple: we couldn't fight against these odds, as they numbered too many.

Jan gazed at our enemies. 'Run lads.'

We fled, Jan bellowing, 'Lads, keep together. Their cavalry won't attack us if we keep shooting at them.'

Every step we took felt like it could be our last. My heart pounded, the blood coursing through my veins. The satisfaction of revenge, the rush of the escape, and the reassurance of our leader all mixed together in a heady stew of passion. The enemy's thundering hooves closed in, but I refused to give up, pushing my legs to move faster, willing myself to outrun them. The wind whipped past my helmet as I ran, the ground a blur beneath my feet. My mail was a heavy burden, and I felt the burn in my muscles, but I didn't slow down. This was a battle for survival, and I would not let them catch me.

The enemy was gaining ground, and if necessary, I would fight until my last breath; in the end, avenging my family was worth it, even if it meant our death. At this point, we no longer ran for our lives, but we ran for our honour, our pride, and our people, single-minded to make it through, no matter the cost.

As we hurtled past Veenkoop, our breaths heaving with effort, we caught a glimpse of our ship looming on the horizon. With no time to spare, we pushed ourselves to the limit, racing to outrun the impending catastrophe. But as we drew closer, another reality hit me with brutal force. Again, we had no time to search for survivors, so any villagers left were on their own now.

As soon as we came into view, Jan's guards readied the ship for boarding. When we arrived, the enemy riders halted, peering at us in silence, our crossbow fire keeping them at a safe distance.

The ship rolled and pitched beneath us when we boarded, our feet slipping on the deck. The wild river crashed against the boat, drenching us while we fired bolts. The wind howled past our helmets, whipping our hair and clothes in all directions. The taste of salt and sweat mixed in my mouth, my heart pounding with the thrill of the fight. The ship creaked and groaned beneath us, tossed around by the raging water.

Winney panicked, her hooves clattering wildly against the wooden deck, eyes wide with fear. The ship rocked violently from side to side, throwing her off balance, causing her to rear up. She searched desperately for a way to escape, but the tightly packed crowd offered no exit.

The enemy infantry closed in yet halted just out of range, content to stare at us from a safe distance. 'You run boy,' Count Floris shouted at me from their ranks. 'These fields are mine now. Tell your bishop that!'

We now sailed away from the shore, but I couldn't help glancing back at him one last time. There, standing tall atop the dykes that had protected me for so many years, stood the enemy leader, beaming. He watched us leave with a calm and collected expression as if he had already won his war against the bishop.

Hate and sorrow swirled inside me. I realised my only refuge was Wiltenburg, where my lord, the bishop, resided. I had to warn him of what had happened on his periphery. Maybe he could send men to retake Veenkoop with me? Maybe other survivors could make their way there too?

The wind in my face, the salty spray of the sea on my skin, and the blood pumping through my veins filled me with a new sense of purpose. While my heart ached beyond understanding, I resolved to make it my life's goal to slay Count Floris one day. I would make it to Wiltenburg, and after that, I would make him pay for what he had done.

Jan restored order to the ship, commanding Rurik to start drumming the rhythm of the waves. Slowly, we coursed the river west, Veenkoop disappearing from sight.

'We will have to sail the seas to the north first and then east to Starum, following the coast line,' he stated. 'That is the safest route, as the count only controls the rivers of the west. He has no reach in northern Frisia, while the bishop has built a line of castles from there all the way to Wiltenburg. From Starum you will be safe to continue on your way Reginhard.'

He put his hand on my shoulder, his face shining in the sunlight. 'I know it is hard now, but give it time and your wounds will heal. The scars, they will remain, but life, your life goes on. Survivors never give up. You must never give up.'

I noticed a small cut on my arm, and as I glanced at it, the day's events flooded my mind. Frethirik came over to me, hugging me like a true brother. The pity on his face as he looked at me only added to my overwhelming sadness. The tears flowed again as we sailed past endless flat fields and dull, brown reeds, each passing day like an eternity of sorrow.

After a few days, we finally reached Starum, yet, the small port did nothing to lift my spirits. The settlement was unremarkable and uninspiring, but I took solace in the fact that it belonged to Count

Bruno, a close ally of our bishop. As we moored at the harbour, despair washed over me when I spotted a half-built mound, similar to Ome Aitet's terp, an agonizing reminder of what we had lost.

The memories of what we had been through, the fear and uncertainty we had faced, all weighed heavily on me. Yet, as we rested in a warm alehouse, rain tapping on the straw roofs, a tiny sense of gratitude for our safety crept in. After drinking a cup of brown ale, I knew I, Frethirik, the longboat's crew, and my horse were finally safe. And the thought of the future, whatever it would hold for us, brought a tiny glimmer of hope to my weary soul.

Chapter Nine

In the morning, Starum's Count Bruno summoned us to his manor, and so Jan, Frethirik, and I strolled our weary feet towards his large hoeve, at least three times the size of my father's. The building towered over us like a fortress, with sturdy timber walls topped by a thatched roof. Small, narrow openings with heavy wooden shutters allowed light and air in while keeping out the wind and rain. The only entrance was a large wooden door guarded by two men armed with swords.

The guards at the entrance waved at Jan, smiles covering their faces. It didn't surprise me since the old captain had a vast network of contacts all along the coast, so I assumed he must have had dealings with the count in the past.

As we entered Starum's great hall, I held my breath in awe. Although the building looked nothing like Thuredrith's towering keep, its lord was no pauper. The massive wooden beams of the ceiling were blackened with age, the sturdy walls adorned by richly coloured tapestries depicting hunting nobles and ancient Frisian battles. Rushes and herbs covered the hall floor, giving off a sweet scent that kept the odor of rotten food and other filth at bay. The fire in the hearth burned brightly, casting a warm glow over the entire hall. Several tables had been set up with platters of food and flagons of ale for the guests to enjoy.

Once inside, I saw several courtiers filling the hall, all dressed in fine wool. The men wore colourful tunics and comfortable leggings, while the women wore long dresses with intricate embroidery.

The count sat on a high seat in the centre of the hall, surrounded by his closest advisors and vassals.

Count Bruno was a large man in his early thirties with a thick brown beard and shoulder-length hair. He wore a yellow cape over a black tunic, attached by a silver clasp. On his fingers, I noticed the glimmer of several silver rings, some embedded with precious stones. He held a silver chalice and inspected some coins, grumbling to the man before him.

Jan bent over to us, whispering quietly. 'The count just minted some new coins. We must wait until he invites us to his side. Keep quiet for now.'

After a few more nods of approval from Count Bruno, he waved away the servant, who quickly closed a chest of silver coins and rushed out through a side door. With the servant gone, Bruno turned his attention towards us, his eyes widening when he spotted Jan. He waved us over, shaking the captain's hand.

'Welcome, my friend. It has been some time since we did business. I still have coin to spare you know, and I happen to be in need of an able captain.' The count paused, remembering that was not why we stood before him. 'Hmmm, forgive me, the harbourmaster told me you are here on a very different account.' He stood, his expression revealing concern. 'Why don't you first tell me what happened near Thuredrith.'

Jan's eyes flicked to the ground. He swallowed hard, his cheeks reddening. 'That Count Floris murdered my friend, my great vrindr in life, Salaco of Veenkoop,' Jan recounted, his mouth twisting. 'He looted and burned the village, taking everything of value, including my own belongings. This young man here,' he continued, pointing at me, 'is Salaco's son and heir, who witnessed his entire family, including his elder brother, slain by Count Floris' men.'

Count Bruno strolled over to me and grabbed my shoulders, his green eyes softening as he looked at me. 'Well, young man, that means the count took lands that belong to the Bishop of Wiltenburg. And that means you have a duty to inform him of this fact.'

'It gets worse,' Jan interjected. 'Somehow Count Floris got the castellan on board, meaning Thuredrith now belongs to Holland too.'

Bruno raised his brows, his eyes widening. 'Damn it, that bloody idiot just sparked a war. He means business with this new Holland he is creating. Just like his brother and father before him. He wants more and more.'

The count swirled around, beckoning to a scribe. Without a moment's pause, he began dictating his message in a rapid stream of words before the servant had even picked up his quill and parchment. The scribe scribbled furiously, struggling to keep up with the count's fast-paced speech.

Bruno then snatched the parchment, rolled it up, and handed it to me. 'Give that to the bishop young man. And make sure you pack up enough food for the journey, because I order you to leave as soon as possible to give word of this outrage to your liege, Bishop William. Now go.'

As we all turned away to leave, Count Bruno settled back in his mighty chair. 'Oh, but Jan. You wait here. I have a little job for you too.' The count's eyes beamed, a grin spreading across his face. 'And it involves those damn Hollanders.'

While Frethirik and I exchanged glances, we said nothing, leaving Jan behind to attend to his task. And as we trotted back, I felt a newfound sense of purpose. My goal was now clear – to meet my liege lord and hopefully gather an army to fight that despicable

Count Floris. I hastened my pace, eager to reach the harbour and prepare for my journey.

Before heading back to the harbour I picked up Winney from the stables. When I returned to the ship, I saw Jan waiting for me.

'What is it, Jan?' I asked, curious to hear what the count wanted from him.

'I'm afraid our paths must part for now, lad,' Jan replied. 'Count Bruno has given us a new task – we are to take on Count Floris' ships near Flardingas. As much as it pains me to leave you, Reginhard, you know I have a responsibility to my men. They need work, food, and silver, so we must set a new course.' He held my shoulders. 'But rest assured, we will never forget what happened. Now you first go and see the bishop. I am sure that at some point we will meet again.'

The captain grabbed my arm, shaking it fiercely. 'God's speed to you on your journey Reginhard.' He then opened my hand, filling it with some silver pennies, certainly enough to pay board for a week.

Trollmann and the men cheered, handing me a bag filled with dried meat, cheese, bread, a waterskin, a woolen blanket, and a warm sheepskin to put over my gambeson. After I hung the bag on Winney's saddle, I turned around to bid farewell to Frethirik. This could be the last time we would see each other for quite a while.

'Good luck fighting that bastard on the sea then, my friend. I am sure we will see each other soon,' I said, trying to hide my sadness.

Frethirik gave me a firm handshake in response, his eyes alight. 'You too Reginhard. Good luck to you. You know you're a great fighter. I am sure the bishop will invite you into his retinue. You'll be fine, my friend.'

Not knowing what else to say, we embraced each other until I finally stepped back. I mounted Winney, and without another word, I set off down the dirt road leading south to Wiltenburg. I waved at the crew until they were no longer in sight, a goodbye to the friends who had saved me from Count Floris's clutches. Now I knew I was truly on my own, my fate taking me to Wiltenburg, the place that would define my future.

The long and winding road led me past rich fields of crops and pastureland on either side. The sun shone brightly in the sky, casting a warm glow on everything around me. Birds sang in the trees, and a light breeze blew through the fields, carrying the scent of freshly cut grass and wildflowers. The Frisian hinterlands were filled with such endless views, while here and there, a small motte signified the presence of a minor ministerial. I had been given enough food for the journey, and Winney rode in good shape, ensuring I moved quickly enough. At times, I needed to ford a river, wetting my boots as we crossed the wild water.

My thoughts kept drifting back to the events that led me to this point. It was hard to believe that just a few days ago, I lived a comfortable life as the son of a ministerial. In the blink of an eye, Count Floris and his dog, Ragnar, took everything I knew and loved.

Still, despite the hardships I now faced, I felt confident the bishop would take me in. My father had always told me that it was my fate to serve the church. As I touched Count Bruno's letter tucked away in my gambeson, I was confident that the bishop would not send a trained warrior away, especially one who had lost everything to Wiltenburg's main enemy.

In the following days, I traveled alone with my thoughts, contemplating what was to come. My only encounters were with traveling merchants and peasants working in the fields. At night, I sought refuge in taverns to rest and have a simple meal. Strangely, despite all the horrors I had experienced and the uncertainty of my future, I slept soundly on the road as if my body had told me I was on the right path. Keeping my focus on reaching my destination, I set out early each day, pushing myself until the last of the daylight had faded.

After three days of travel, the road brought me to the outskirts of Wiltenburg. A deep nostalgia crept over me as I looked upon the town appearing on the horizon, for I had returned to my birthplace. In the middle of the flat fields, with bleating sheep grazing nearby, stood the pearl of the Frisian lowlands – its stout wooden walls adorned with the red and white banners of the bishopric. This was where I was raised when my father was still active as a household warrior in the bishop's personal guard.

I approached the town's massive gates, where two guards inspected the many merchants and commoners passing through, seeming incredibly alert to danger. When I handed Count Bruno's letter to a grey-haired warrior, he brushed his mustache at the sight of the letter's seal. 'So you come from the court of Count Bruno, young man?' he inquired.

'Yes master guard. In fact, I hail from Veenkoop, near Thuredrith. A few days ago, I saw how the castellan betrayed our lord bishop, handing the town to Count Floris of Holland. I am here on urgent business, to inform his lordship of these events immediately.'

The veteran's eyes widened. 'Well young man, I will tell you something then. You are not the first soul to enter our gates with this news. Another from your village came here last evening, distraught and famished. He damn well told us the same news. That is why we inspect all who enter our gates with extra care. The Count of Holland just declared war on us.'

The veteran gestured to a young guard, who ran over to him. 'Rolf, you must escort this young man to the bishop's palace immediately,' he said. 'Tell them that he has news from Thuredrith. Go now!'

Without delay, Rolf took hold of my reins, spurring us into the town. Rushing through the gates, my mind wondered: Who had managed to arrive? Could it have been Gerold? Had he truly escaped? The uncertainty of my future only added to the weight of the painful news I carried, so I braced myself for whatever lay ahead. Little did I know that this was the beginning of a long, dangerous road.

Chapter Ten

As we passed through the gates, I was transported back to my childhood. The first thing that caught my eye was the bustling common area, where warehouses, cellars, market stalls, and burgher residences stood tall and proud. It hadn't changed a bit.

My gaze was drawn to the quaint Buurchurch, its steeple towering high into the sky. We always had to listen to mass quietly or risk Father's stiff reprimands. The area around the church was as alive with activity as it was back then, with merchants and labourers going about their daily business. They stored goods in their various warehouses, where cool cellars provided a refuge for food and drinks.

We trudged through the market stalls, where vendors shouted and haggled over the freshest produce. Over the stalls towered proud burgher residences, some even radiating their owner's status with precious, ornamental saints on their walls. I thanked God, feeling very grateful to be home – back in a place where I belonged.

After passing the common area, we reached a fortified part of town separated by a bridge, where the bishop lived. As we passed through Wiltenburg's gate, I glanced at a massive building right next to a tower, which I knew was the imperial palace of Lofen, where the emperor resided during visits.

The palace was a stunning sight to behold. Intricate carvings adorned its grand façade, while tall columns rose up to support the imposing roof. Lush gardens and fountains surrounded the palace, creating a serene environment amidst the bustling city, such a contrast to the common area. Of course, while the emperor only occasionally visited the castle, its presence symbolized our empire's power and wealth.

Two guards stationed at the palace gates stood like statues, their gaze fixed upon the entrance. The imperial colours of black and yellow were brightly displayed on their kite shields; they were a formidable sight to behold. When we approached, the guards recognised Rolf and immediately allowed us to pass on to the Bishop's tower.

The tall tower cast a dark shadow over us, blocking out the sun to dwindle us in its presence. As we neared, a group of people were in a heated argument. Among them was an authoritarian noble, his rich garments and wild gestures marking him as a person of high status. He addressed a crowd of men in front of a large, intricately carved wooden statue depicting a monk.

'I have no concern for any of the residences outside this stronghold. The count of Holland is becoming increasingly aggressive, and I am solely responsible for the defense of Wiltenburg.' The commanding figure stared at a modest-looking man with a round face and an even rounder belly.

'Lord, I understand your point completely, but as a representative of the merchants I must protest. Tearing down the warehouses and residences outside the stronghold means that a part of the town's wealth will disappear.'

The merchant frowned slightly at the tone of his own message. 'And with all due respect my lord, that also means the bishop will have less tariffs coming in.'

The noble shook his head. 'I don't care man. If this town gets taken by the count, his rampaging Danes or Flemish or whatever other filth he hires, that is what will destroy all of your homes and businesses.'

He waved the man away. 'You mind your little wares, merchant, and I will do my job as viscount. As saint Willibrord is my witness.' He faced the statue, making the sign of the cross.

He pointed at the gate of the fort. 'All right boys, I want to reinforce the wall there, there and there.'

As my guide and I continued to make our way to the tower, I reflected on the viscount's warnings. It was clear that Wiltenburg was already preparing for a full-scale war against Count Floris, warned by the person from my village. So, who had made it here before me?

I didn't have to wait long for an answer. When Rolf banged on the tower's gate, a hatch opened. A lone eye scrutinised us from head to toe, a sour voice murmuring something barely audible.

'I told you earlier, merchant filth, the bishop will not see you right now. He is praying and cannot be disturbed!'

I furrowed my brow. Meanwhile, the guardsman responded, 'it is Rolf, Sir Deacon, from the gate. I have brought a man who says he has news of Thuredrith. He says he was there when they took the bishop's lands.'

I bowed deeply to the eye peering at me through the hatch. 'I am no merchant, sir. My name is Reginhard, son of Salaco. He was appointed ministerial of Veenkoop after serving as Bishop Bernold's household warrior.'

Examining me from head to toe, I heard a sniff and a low rumbling noise until the dark door creaked open a fraction of an inch. 'Well, what are you waiting for? Move your arse and come in. We don't want a dozen burghers disrupting our prayers. Never do their endless requests stop.'

Assured by Rolf that Winney would be taken to the stable, I dismounted and rushed into the tower, the door shutting behind me in full force. Looking around, I stood in a large room bustling with activity.

Various priests, deacons, monks, and even nuns scurried about their business as if the devil himself chased them. And it hardly took me two breaths to realise why they were all so diligently engaged in their chores. A harsh command penetrated the clergy's activities.

A fox-faced figure appeared from some red curtains, strolling into the room with a frustrated step. Clearly of noble birth, he had a regal bearing and was draped in an opulent woolen garment woven with gold thread, the fabric heavy and luxurious. The sleeves were wide and billowing, and the hem was trimmed with elegant fur. The figure's features were sharp, with piercing eyes that commanded attention.

His gaze swept the surrounding area as he stood before the throne, taking it in with practiced ease. It was evident that this was someone of great importance, and his presence added to the already grand atmosphere of the room. It could only be one man then, I thought. This had to be bishop William.

He addressed a priest clad in a black robe who tried to avoid the bishop's gaze. 'What did you mean, Father Rembrand, when you wrote only two pounds of silver could be extracted from Tiel? My estimates told me they were to pay four pounds of silver. Four! Which is supposed to be twice the amount you brought back.'

I felt terrible for this priest, who now winced, bowing deeply. 'Truly, my lord bishop, Tiel's ministerial assured me that was all they could spare this season.'

Bishop William's face twitched. 'You were armed with my guards and still you fell for the lies of those snakes?' The fox-like features transformed into those of a wolf, the rapid change strangely seamless. 'You turd, you will haul your pitiful carcass back there immediately. You will not return until you present me with my proper share of the taxes.' This Father Rembrand, his head hung low, nodded, speeding past me.

The bishop now addressed the whole gathering. 'In Heaven's name, how can everyone here suffer from sloth!' I winced, looking around me – every serf in the diocese must have heard him. The red-eyed stare moved from frozen face to frozen face, pausing sometimes longer, sometimes shorter, until it finally rested on me.

I felt very uncomfortable. Through his stare, I was reminded of all my terrible sins, and I tried to avoid looking down the moment he locked his gaze on me. Instead, manning up, I faced his force as my guide started addressing his superior.

'Dear Bishop William. This here lad says he is the son of a certain Salaco, my lord, one who had served in our holy father Bernold's guard.' The deacon made the sign of the cross, touching his fingers to his head, chest, and shoulders as if to ensure even the Good Father in Heaven heard him speak the truth.

The bishop frowned. 'So what's your story, lad? You the second son of another spoiled farmer or other?'

Before I could answer, he spoke again. 'The arrogance most of these scum have nowadays. There is simply no respect anymore for their betters, their leaders in life, their guides to the Gates of Heaven. Except we cannot guide them to heaven, for they possess only vice.'

He sighed. 'It almost seems as if the silver ends up in the ministerial's pockets.' The bishop shook his head. 'Well never mind for now. So young man do you have any papers to prove who you are?'

Already holding my papers in hand, now bowing as deeply as possible, I tried to appease him with Count Bruno's letter. 'Yes, my liege, I have it right here.'

As the bishop read the letter, his brows furrowed deeply. 'Well, Count Bruno brings dire news for sure. So, you were present when the attack occurred?'

I nodded, my eyes darting to the floor, the painful memories again emerging from the corners of the dark room. I swallowed, fighting to gain control. I had to man up and give the bishop the facts.

Bishop William grunted. 'And you now wish to complete your training here in my army, becoming part of my retinue.'

I nodded my head once more, bowing.

'It can be arranged,' he stated briskly, almost carelessly. 'But you must provide your own armour, horses and weapons.' Waving, he added, 'first follow me young man and explain in detail all that you experienced. Then let us work out what to do from there.'

He led us behind the curtains to some stairs, which led us to a private room where we could speak freely without any courtiers overhearing. I recounted all that had happened, and the bishop now listened attentively, without interruption, until I finished.

The bishop's back was turned towards me as he stared outside, fumbling his chin for a while. 'All right lad. You will receive lodgings here as a miles and you will be appointed a mentor that will teach you the military arts. As much as it saddens me, this world still needs its crude warrior servants, and to be honest you fit the bill perfectly.'

While keeping a stony face on the surface, my heart leapt with joy. 'Thank you, Bishop William. Thank you.' The prospect of completing my training under his command filled me with an excitement I struggled to contain. I bowed deeply, unsure of what else to say.

The bishop gestured for a servant, who led me out of the tower to a modest barracks area. As we walked, I kept my head low and followed in silence, my thoughts spinning. When we arrived at my quarters, I couldn't help but feel a twinge of disappointment at the simple and damp space I was shown. It was located near the stables and hardly seemed like a place of comfort. Still, I reminded myself that having a roof over my head and a place within the walls of a lord was a blessing in itself. With a quick sign of the cross, I silently thanked God for this turn of fate.

I sat on the simple straw bed, lost in deep contemplation, until a knock on the door jolted me out of my thoughts. Startled, I turned around and leaped up from the bed. To my amazement, Gerold stood in the doorway, his eyes gleaming. I mirrored his expression, hurrying to embrace him tightly.

Now in tears, Gerold explained how he had reached Wiltenburg on foot, having marched all the way there, asking directions from peasants and villagers. 'The monks just told me I now am to serve you again, young lord. Then the stable boy gave me a place next to Winney,' he said.

Overwhelmed with gratitude, I accepted his service at once. Then I watched as he moved my possessions into my quarters, including my valuable mail armour, kite shield with the twin fish emblem, and iron sword. With the last silver left, I decided to treat us to some good ale and share tales of how we had survived. That night, we toasted on better days to come.

Chapter Eleven

The next day, I was introduced to my new fighting instructor, a man called Robert. Gerold led me to the training fields, where I spotted a tall, muscular man in his early forties hammering a dummy with a wooden sword. Beardless, with short, dark hair and only a faint touch of grey on his temples, he wore only breeches and boots. I was struck by how much he resembled my father from a distance.

When we neared him, I noticed he wore several scars on his body, with an especially pronounced one decorating his cheek, clearly the result of years of fighting. Gerold told me he was a Norman who had pledged himself to the bishop's service after receiving healing from the bishop's physicians. Robert apparently had years of experience in battle and a deep understanding of the art of combat.

When I introduced myself, Robert simply shrugged, continuing to hammer the dummy with his wooden sword. 'Well, welcome then, Reginhard of Veenkoop. I've already heard a thing or two about you.' He gestured for me to join him in the ring and pointed to a wooden sword waiting for me. Without wasting any more words, he just indicated we start. I had to prove myself now, I thought.

He took his stance, the same drill sergeant stance my father always used. I breathed out, calming my nerves. Just do what Father taught you, I thought, slowly starting to circle him.

'So what's this,' Robert grumbled, furrowing his brow. 'You look like you have seen some bits of this world already. I can see it in a man's eyes you know. Yours portray sorrow and hardship.' He nodded. 'Show me what you got then boy.'

I swung my blade around to test its balance before lunging. However, Robert just stepped aside, tripping me with his leg, causing me to lose balance.

Shaking my head, I again took the battle stance. Robert smiled, then lunged at me with ferocious speed. He came at me, hammering the heavy wooden sword, making me parry, parry again, and block. His relentless attacks forced me to defend with all my might, my arms aching from the effort, sweat dripping from my forehead. Despite my best efforts, Robert quickly found openings in my defense, striking me lightly but consistently.

'Fine footing lad, but still, much could be improved.' He snorted. 'Basics are there, but even with basics a trained warrior will take your life in a blink.' He clicked his fingers, kicking me in the groin. I winced, but his blade was already pointed at my face before I could react.

'Dead!' he said flatly.

That was how it all started, and for the next few weeks, my days were shaped by repetitive hours of training. From dawn to noon, Robert drilled me relentlessly, pushing me to my limits. During the breaks, Gerold would arrive with food and water for us, and after the break, we resumed training until dusk. The same grueling punishment day in, day out.

Yet, as time passed, Robert became more than just my instructor. He became my mentor, my friend, and even a little like a father. I learned so much from him, not just about fighting and survival but also about life. He taught me what it meant to be a good person, how to deal with loss, and how to find meaning and purpose in life.

Under his guidance, I grew physically stronger, focused, and more disciplined. I no longer saw training as a punishment but as an opportunity to improve and become a better warrior. And as I made progress, I gained the respect of my fellows. They no longer saw me as the inexperienced boy from Veenkoop but as a dedicated warrior in the making. Slowly, steadily, I was earning my place among the warriors of Wiltenburg.

In truth, those weeks became a period of healing for me. Under Robert's guidance, I learned to organise my thoughts and find the balance between my training goals and personal grief. And whenever the sadness or the anger surfaced, I confided in Gerold. Although he didn't say much, he understood what I was going through, having experienced the same horrors himself. In fact, he was a great comfort to me as we both learned to acknowledge the dreadful events of the early spring. Although we neither forgot nor forgave, for now, we moved forward.

Yet, after a month of rigorous training, there was still no command to retake Veenkoop or fight Count Floris, which irritated me. Also, I would never find true acceptance among the men until I proved myself in battle. I wanted to take on the Hollanders. I wanted revenge and action.

Finally, a message came, and Robert and I were called for an audience by the bishop. As we were led to his private room, he sat ready for us on a luxurious chair. It was as if he now had a small throne, the handles representing various saints, and the back of his seat shaped like a cross. I couldn't help but stare in awe, which prompted Bishop William, smiling broadly, to start a lecture.

'It is a wonder, isn't it, young Reginhard?' he said. 'This chair helps to place me in the position of our Lord Jesus Christ. When I sit on it, it reminds me to act according to his gracious example.'

As the bishop continued, my attention drifted towards the large tapestries adorning the walls. The intricate designs and vibrant colours captured my imagination, the battles depicted on them reminding me of my forefathers. Despite nodding politely, my thoughts continued to drift.

Finished with his lesson, the bishop pointed at the most magnificent tapestry in the room, depicting a holy man from Britain named Willibrord. Its sophisticated details caught my eye, the artistry that had gone into creating it impressing me greatly. The vivid and bright colours are intricately interwoven, giving rise to numerous detailed images that effortlessly draw you into the captivating beauty of the piece. Willibrord stood in the centre, surrounded by the miracles of his life. I gaped at the lifelike quality of the images and the way the weaver had captured the essence of the holy man's character, my reaction clearly satisfying the bishop, who started smiling again.

'Did you know, Reginhard, that the Saxons from Britain have been a great help in bringing the Lord's message to the ignorant Frisian pagans here?' The bishop asked, raising his brows. 'The holy Willibrord, you see, was in fact the first officially sanctioned bishop in these parts and had his seat right here in Wiltenburg.'

When I shook my head, the bishop started pacing up and down the room, launching into a new lecture. To my deep regret, some of his spittle found its way to my face now and then, but I did my best to remain polite and attentive, chiming in with 'yes, my lord' and 'amen, Bishop William.' He preached for a while until a change in his tone caught me off guard. He suddenly faced me and offered condolences for my loss. It felt strange coming from him, and, at first, I wasn't sure if he genuinely meant it. Did he have ulterior motives? Yet, his calm gaze reassured me that he was genuine.

'I appreciate your kind words, Bishop William,' I replied, trying to keep my voice steady. 'I have been doing my best to cope and move forward with the help of my companions.'

'But, my lord,' I continued, 'while I do feel better now, I still haven't forgotten how some sea raiders, led by a Ragnar Ivarson, burned Veenkoop and killed my family, all on the orders of Count Floris.'

The bishop winced, hissing, 'Yes, Floris had the audacity to lend that area to a freeman.'

It took a moment to process this new information, but honestly, it made perfect sense. My family had never been on good terms with Count Floris, so he simply seized the opportunity to remove us from our land and replace us with someone loyal to him. Admittedly, it was a shrewd move.

'Well,' the bishop's voice beamed again. 'You are now in my service and I have no doubt that you will flourish here, as long as you conduct yourself as a proper Christian.' He then picked up a quill and a piece of parchment. 'Now, I probably already know the answer to this, but can you read and write, young man?'

'Yes, lord, my father hired a scribe to teach me the basics.' Bishop William's eyebrows shot up. Even Robert grunted in disbelief. 'That is not something I often hear, young Reginhard,' the bishop exclaimed. 'A ministerial's son who writes. Hah, well, if you ever attain the status of an officer, this skill will come in handy.' Bishop William scribbled on, leaving us waiting for further instructions.

'In fact, Reginhard, it will come in handy for the important task I have for you both.' I held my breath. What did he mean? Would we finally take back Veenkoop and Thuredrith?

'As you can appreciate, attempting to take back Thuredrith

now would be folly,' Bishop William explained, a servant suddenly pouring us some wine, an extreme luxury. My heart sank again, and my head hung low. Of course, I knew that Bishop Bernold had only succeeded in conquering Thuredrith in the past after the emperor reinforced our army.

'No, we must wait for a better opportunity to strike.' The bishop added, his eyes still on the parchment. I lowered my eyes. I had waited weeks to get back at Count Floris, constantly questioning Robert for news of the high command. Now, clearly, this would take a lot longer than I hoped. But why did the bishop summon us then?

Bishop William stood up, facing the window. He took a deep sip of wine, his gaze now fixed on the lush gardens outside. 'As you both know, the Saxons played a significant role in spreading Christianity throughout these lands. And you're probably familiar with how Holy Willibrord was appointed as the first bishop of Wiltenburg . . . ,' he said, his voice trailing off. Pausing for a moment, the bishop looked up at the ceiling as if searching for the saint himself. 'I had a vision that revealed how you will assist Wiltenburg with a great task. A mighty task. One that, if you succeed, will shape your fates and reward you beyond your wildest dreams.'

Landing back into his chair, he faced us again, raising a hand toward the heavens. 'I heard the Lord's name prophesize a great deed! And you two are to play a part in it. Reginhard, Robert. You are to travel to England to reclaim one of Willibrord's relics, his most holy ring, to finally return it to its rightful place here.' He slammed his fist on the table. 'Hah, those damned clerics from Echternach claim they have all his relics, and a great many pilgrims visit that monastery each year. They grow rich and fat on the backs of us Wiltenburg men.' He sighed deeply. 'As you probably know,

I have a new building project in mind. But of course, I cannot rebuild the Salvator Church without adding a precious relic of our forefather to it.'

Robert glanced at me with open eyes, his brows raised. 'But sire, where are we to start? How do we even know where to look for such a relic?'

Bishop William grinned at the veteran. 'Good of you to ask Robert. It is true that I do not know precisely where the ring is right now. Yet I just received some information from my agent in Echternach.'

A spy, I thought.

The bishop chuckled. 'It seems the abbot discovered a letter in his ancient monastery that reveals that one crucial relic was sent back to Bishop Willibrord's home country of England when the saint died. 'Yet, what he is not aware of is that I know his secret too, and I happen to have a connection there, good Bishop Æthelmaer of Elmham.' The bishop's eyes sparkled. 'So the hunt is on, gentlemen. The hunt is on.'

William leaned back into his chair, his voice settling into a more measured tone. 'It is probable, according to Bishop Æthelmaer, that the ring was lost during the pagan invasions of England more than a century ago. He advised me to send you to the region of East Anglia. From there, he can assist you in locating the relic. In exchange for his help, I agreed to provide him with some labourers, and chests of silver. To that end, I have arranged for ships to transport you and some Frisian settlers to Bishop Æthelmaer. The ship departs at noon tomorrow, so you should prepare for your journey now. The servants will have food and your horses ready at dawn.'

Bishop William clapped his hands, smiling again. 'You will be, as our Holy Father, Pope Victor, calls it, true Miles Christi!'

The bishop made the sign of the cross, waving his hand to dismiss us. As we left, Robert sighed. 'This won't be easy you know. These Echternach monks will have sent their own men to England. And they'll get there before us.'

We raced back to our barracks to pack our belongings, and I wondered what kind of strange journey awaited me now. Fate was a cruel mistress, and my revenge had to wait. For now, England waited for us.

Chapter Twelve

The next morning, we stood ready to depart, with Gerold packing the last of our food. The bishop had sent another servant to assist Robert, but he stubbornly declined, waving the man back to the tower.

'Servant are for lords,' the Norman grunted. 'And until I am elevated to one I take care of my own armour and weapons.'

I just shrugged, happy to have Gerold help us with our belongings, and besides, we had grown very close together in the past weeks, the whole situation in Wiltenburg new for us both. It felt nice to have Gerold along, the only soul I had left from Veenkoop.

As the morning clouds slowly dissipated, a sunny summer day welcomed our departure to Starum. The journey to the port didn't take long, the weather treating us with kindness. Two days later, we approached the small harbour of the village.

A surprise waited for us upon our arrival. My heart leapt at the sight of Jan, Trollmann, and Frethirik welcoming us onto the wharf. I couldn't believe we were together again.

They embraced me, their hands patting my back, their boisterous laughter ringing in my ears. They had not changed since the last time I saw them, and their rough-and-tumble appearance brought a smile to my face. 'What are all of you doing here then?'

Jan grinned widely. 'Your bishop hired us to transport two warriors and a colony of Frisian settlers to East-Anglia. Ha, you should have seen Frethirik's face when he heard it was the young man from Veenkoop we were ordered to pick up.'

I introduced my friends to Robert and Gerold, everyone shaking hands. Jan led us to his ship, showing us his new crew members, all young men eager to see the world and fight for silver.

We spent the rest of the evening reminiscing about the old days. It was as if no time had passed, and I felt grateful to have my old friends back. The prospect of setting sail with them again filled me with excitement – another thrilling journey about to begin. After I told them about our mission of finding Saint Willibrord's ring, Jan explained that the Frisian settlers joining us were to clear some land for Bishop Æthelmaer of Elmham.

'And you know what that means Reginhard. Just how Bishop Bernold profited from your father.' Jan fumbled a silver denar from his pocket. 'The Bishop of Elmham will of course tax these new settlers.'

Trollmann pointed at the raised earthworks on the edge of Starum. 'He also requires their expertise in dyke building, as East-Anglia is filled with swamps and rivers.'

The following day, feeling well-rested, we set off on our journey. We boarded the snekkja while Winney and Robert's horse joined a group of settlers, some twenty in number, aboard a spacious cog with all their equipment, tools, animals, and belongings.

Jan grumbled about how he hardly got paid for this journey. 'But when we heard you were the one they were going to need protection for, we immediately signed up at the harbour master. We're only here to protect the settlers, something they normally hire a crew on board for.' He shrugged, adding, 'Ah well, I happen to know the thegn that rules that harbour town. And I am sure he'll have some work for us.'

The sun began to rise, and we said goodbye to the shores of Frisia. The crew worked quickly to cast off the lines and hoist the sails. As the wind picked up and filled the sails, our ship glided through the water, propelling us out to sea. I stood at the railing, mesmerised by the beauty of the sunrise and the peacefulness of the sea. At that moment, it felt like a fresh start, as if we could leave behind our past experiences and embark on a new adventure. The thought of it exhilarated me, and with Jan, Trollmann, Frethirik, and the rest of the crew by my side, anything was possible.

Yet only two days later, after a windy night rocked the ship to and fro, my excitement faded. Sick to my bones, melancholy gripped my soul as the memories of Ragnar Ivarson's men haunted my dreams day and night. At night, I stood on the ship's prow, watching the waves dance in the rhythm of the sea. I looked up, seeking solace from Heaven. Countless stars dotted the sky, lighting up our path to England.

'It's a good night for thought and memory.' Trollmann, his pale face ghoulish in the dark, came to my side and put his shoulder over me.

'I realised that I have not properly offered my condolences concerning your family and what Ragnar Ivarson did to you Reginhard.'

His words caused a sharp pang in my chest.

'I try not to think about it much anymore Trollmann.' I forced myself to shrug. 'Thank you,' I managed to respond at last.

He nodded. 'You know, it is not always bad to remember wrongs done to you. Sometimes, through hardships, we learn lessons too. Learn how to survive.'

'Why? Did you lose someone, Trollmann?'

Behind the warm expression of the Sami warrior, an unexpected revelation emerged. 'My people, Reginhard, have faced something very similar to the Frisians.'

I shook my head. 'But I thought your tribe came from Norway and that you were just another warrior in Jan's company,' I responded, surprised by his comparison.

'It is not entirely true. My people are actually hunters, who roam from place to place in the frozen wastelands of the true north.' Shrill resentment blended into Trollmann's sympathetic voice. 'And we have suffered for a while now.'

Trollmann recalled how King Cnut once came to Trondheim, one of Norway's most northern trading towns. 'He was a powerful lord, leading an empire of many lands across several seas. But he wanted more, and so he subdued Norway.'

My eyes widened. 'Yes, I have heard of this man Trollmann. My grandfather often told tales of his wealth and his honour,' I replied. 'He was a Viking lord, my grandfather said.'

'That he was, Reginhard, that he was, and not at all fond of the Sami.' He sighed. 'We just wanted freedom, but like the Frisians, couldn't obtain it. He saw to that all right.'

'It all started when our tribe stopped supplying the Norse with pelts. They had allowed us to live in peace on our hunting grounds if we provided pelts and meat as tax. But one winter,' Trollmann paused, on old pain surfacing on his tight cheeks.

'One winter it was just so cold that we didn't even have enough food for our own people. It was then that a number of men from Trondheim came to our village to demand what they saw as taxes they were owed. They took some of our women and said they would take more slaves if we would not provide them with their rightful share of goods and food.' Trollmann paused again, staring at the stars.

'They took my woman too.' Trollmann continued, his eyes darkening into ash. 'I couldn't just sit there and do nothing, so, me and a couple of our men decided to retaliate against the local jarl. Luring them back in the pretense of paying the demanded taxes, we planned our revenge. We waited for them in the deep forest of our frozen Lapland, and when the time was right, we took them down one by one. A brutal act for sure, but we felt we had no other choice.'

Trollmann's gaze turned back to mine. 'A mistake, of course, as King Cnut soon heard of our transgressions and came with a force of warriors to avenge his slain subordinates. They stormed into our village, slaughtered all the reindeer, and took every single soul prisoner.'

Trollmann grabbed an alesack and took a long drink before continuing. 'Since I was the leader of the party that had ambushed the Jarl, my children got taken from me.' Trollmann winced, his voice now trembling. 'In front of everyone.' Trollmann took a moment to regain control of his voice. 'Have you ever heard of the blood eagle Reginhard?'

I shook my head, thinking that sounded right pagan.

'It's one of the worst deaths that the Norse inflict on prisoners and enemies that have betrayed them. They took both my young children and started cutting into their backs, taking out their lungs while they still lived. Then they threw them off the boats to make them fly, drowning them in that state.'

Another silence, Trollmann's cheeks tightening again. 'Afterwards they took me prisoner, forcing me to fight for the Norse, half a slave, until one of our boats capsized in a storm one day. I washed up on the West-Frisian coast, where I met Jan. Since that day I fought for booty and nothing but blood.'

He grabbed the amulet hanging from his neck. 'Yet then, one day, Jan sailed us to a magnificent place on the very edge of our world. After years of sailing as a ghost, with no other passion than slaughter and no other reality than the wide seas of the north, I finally found peace in this paradise called Iceland.' Trollmann glanced north, a smile gradually forming on his tight lips. 'There, Reginhard, a man can truly find peace. A place where the gods walk among the mortals, where the earth spews fire into the lakes, and the fairies dance in the green skies of Valhalla. Never have I seen a place on earth where Man stands so close to the gods. It was as if they were all there again; my wife with me in the warm baths of the central mountains and my children singing to me as I rode through the endless pastures of Reykjavik.'

Trollmann put a hand on my shoulder. 'You'll be all right Reginhard.'

I swept away a tear, praying such a fate would never befall my future family. However much I had already suffered, his experience proved much worse, our world making some endure even greater evils than the count of Holland.

Lost in thought for the next few miles, I simply watched the stars, reflecting on God's intentions. The waters of the sea had calmed now, glistening in the starlight. Yet, as I peered forward, I noticed something in the distance. It took a while until I was sure. I had spotted the English coast, rising from the earth like Adam. Squinting to make sure, I realised this was it; we must finally have arrived at our destination. England stood right there in front of us.

Chapter Thirteen

'Jan, Frethirik, Trollmann. Land ahead!'

My heart raced as I heard the call of Jan, Frethirik, and Trollmann echo my announcement across the two ships. I had dreamt of this journey for years, even before it had become a concrete mission, and the excitement of finally setting foot in a foreign land was almost too much to bear.

As we approached the shore, I glimpsed England, this land that I had heard so much about. The sea air smelled crisp and salty, with seagulls protesting our arrival above us, cackling their warnings.

The shoreline now came into view, with rolling hills and meadows, the landscape lush and green. I grabbed Frethirik's sleeve to point at a fox escaping into some woods. I couldn't wait to explore this new land, immerse myself in its culture and learn about its people.

Our ships calmly sailed into the mouth of a wide river, Jan declaring that we had safely reached England. Yet since it was still dark, we had to stop at the river's bank, the captain deciding it was too dangerous to sail the river at night. As we disembarked, my heart swelled. Eager to begin my adventure in this mysterious country, I couldn't stop thinking about our mission, exhilaration coursing through my veins. I knew we had to move quickly to the port town of Ipswich and ask its lord the whereabouts of this Bishop of Elmsham. We just had to get to Willibrord's ring before the agents of Echternach could.

But now it was dark, and our party had to rest for a bit, so upon our arrival on land, Jan promptly ordered me and Frethirik to gather firewood for the night. Craving to settle down and fill our bellies, we quickly grabbed an axe, trudging into a nearby patch of woods.

As we crossed through the woodland looking for suitable branches, the stars cast a silver glow over the trees. Although it was early summer, the night air was still cool. The forest pulsed with the sounds of nature, the rustling of leaves, and the occasional snap of a twig. The smell of pine and damp earth was strong, reminding me of the many hunting trips I had enjoyed in Veenkoop.

When we made our way deeper into the woodland in search of larger chunks of wood, the serenity of the forest calmed my nerves. Even in the dark, I could appreciate how the trees stood tall and majestic, reaching towards the sky like giants to surround us in the beauty of the wild.

We worked together to gather the firewood, the sounds of our axes cutting through the branches echoing through the forest. The smell of freshly cut timber filled our nostrils, my satisfaction building as we stacked the wood neatly.

'And, what do you think of this place called East Anglia?' Frethirik inquired of me in his usual derisive tone.

'Well, so far it is not that much different from home. But honestly my mind is completely focused on our mission right now. Just think of the rewards we could get from our bishop.'

Dreaming about piles of silver, I took a large branch from the forest floor, hacking off a chunk. 'Let's just get on with this so we can eat. I'm starving.'

At that point, I did most of the hard work, Frethirik's lazy arse not moving an inch anymore. It seemed he decided he had to share a tale about a Starum wench he had chased after for some months, clearly more important than the firewood. I paused, grabbing my alesack to oblige my friend's enthusiasm. Maybe his story would include some entertaining details about him getting rejected.

But as he chatted on and on, the boredom crept in. Just as I was nodding off, my companion suddenly announced that he urgently needed to answer the call of nature. Without hesitation, he scampered off behind some nearby trees. As he disappeared from view, I made a hasty retreat in the opposite direction, eager to avoid his lovely pink buttocks.

Yet, as soon as I started to relax in a new spot, I glimpsed a movement out of the corner of my eye. I peered into the darkness just as a glint of metal whizzed past me. I heard a sharp metallic tang, my heart now pounding rapidly in my chest.

Another arrow drilled into the oak tree next to my face. We were under attack. There was no time to warn Frethirik as a screaming warrior rushed toward me, a club in hand.

He lunged. I blocked his strike with my axe, the sound of the weapons ringing out into the night. I could feel the force of his attack reverberate through my arms, but I stood my ground, refusing to give an inch. With my opponent's surprise thwarted, I launched a counter-attack. Bringing my axe down with all my might, I aimed for his foot, the blade sinking deep into flesh and bone. A cry of pain pierced the night as my foe stumbled backward. I stood over him, my axe at the ready, watching as he clutched his injured foot, whimpering.

Despite the violence, a certain satisfaction washed over me. I survived a surprise attack and now had the power to end this man's life. It felt good.

I raised my axe just as something whizzed past my arm, missing me by inches. Without thinking, I dropped behind a nearby bush, scanning for any signs of my new attacker. At a sudden movement to my left, I sprang into action, dashing into the woods to flank my assailant.

With the thick undergrowth, I had to fight through tangled brambles and branches as I moved deeper into the forest. Confronting my attacker head-on was a considerable risk, but I had to try. 'When facing an ambush, do the unexpected,' my father would say. 'Always take the initiative.'

As I battled through the thick foliage, something else caught my eye. It was Frethirik, swinging a massive branch with some kind of brown substance on it. His target was a pox-ridden individual in tattered brown rags. The bandit got blinded by the odiferous matter, allowing Frethirik to strike him repeatedly with his makeshift weapon. Blow after blow rained down on the hapless attacker until he finally fell to the ground, motionless.

But my relief proved short-lived. I now closed in on the archer, who brandished a knife, swinging it at my throat. Intuitively, I raised my heavy axe, blocking the attack in time. Yet the archer proved agile, feinting to one side and then making a sharp move to the other, cutting my arm. I struggled to maintain my grip on my weapon, and he kicked the handle of my axe out of my hand.

I was in serious trouble with my weapon lying uselessly on the ground. The archer advanced on me, knife at the ready, while I braced myself for the worst. Though determined to keep fighting, no matter what it took, I suddenly felt this might be the end. I cried my lungs out, but at that moment, my body somehow took over. My arm moved of its own accord, drawing my knife and swinging it at the archer's face.

Despite his quick reactions, I managed to land a glancing blow, causing him to stumble back. He quickly regained his footing and grabbed my arm, holding it tightly. In a struggle for our lives, we held onto each other with all our strength.

The world around us faded, leaving us locked in a desperate fight for survival. Every muscle in my body tensed as I fought to break free from the archer's grip, knowing that the slightest mistake could be fatal. The putrid smell of the archer's breath filled my nostrils, and I saw broken, yellow teeth in his rancid mouth. The stench was overpowering, and I momentarily lost focus. The archer took advantage of my momentary weakness and nearly threw me onto the forest floor. But, I twisted my body, regaining my footing.

The fight seemed to last for an eternity, each of us giving as much as we got until I finally managed to wrench my arm free from the archer's grip, sending him stumbling backwards. For a moment, we both stood there, catching our breath. With a last, triumphant cry, I raised my hand high, ready to finish off my defeated foe once and for all.

Grabbing his weapon, I drove it into his thigh. He cried out, clutching at the wound – his face twisted, his breathing laboured. I sighed. Being a trained and well-fed warrior was the only reason I survived that contact. Robert's training had pulled me through, and I quickly whispered a prayer of thanks for him and the Lord above. Then, I picked up my axe, ending his life in a painful but deserving death.

Looking up from my victory, I saw Frethirik battling the first man I had wounded. My friend's foot, spit and strikes rained down on the small bandit, who eventually succumbed to the beating. Then, Frethirik waved his axe ceremoniously above his wounded enemy. And with a primal scream, he ended another life deemed worthless.

'Bloody hell,' my friend breathed as I approached. 'I can finally finish my shit in peace now.'

I raised my brows. He had clearly killed men in his recent sea adventures as he went about his business as calmly as he had been yapping at me before. Yet, realising that I had just taken a life meant a moment of clarity. Despite the feeling of satisfaction, I had been lucky to have survived such a dangerous battle. It could be my blood spilling across the ground, my unfocused eyes staring towards the heavens.

'No coin or nothing on 'em,' Frethirik grunted, pissing on the bandit's face. 'There, take that with ye to Hell!'

As I gazed at my opponent's lifeless body, I wondered, Why did it happen? Who were these people?

Chapter Fourteen

As we made our way back to camp, despite being covered in the grime and sweat of battle, pride accompanied our step. The twigs and branches crackling underfoot sounded like a chorus celebrating our victory. Our breath came in heavy gasps, our hearts beating loudly as we relived what just happened.

When we approached the campfire, the smell of wood smoke greeted us. Burning some small twigs, the crew jumped up when they saw us, their eyes widening. Jan ran over to us. 'What the hell happened to you?' He led us to the firepit, where Trollmann put down a bucket of water for us, handing us an alesack each.

As we settled around the campfire, roasting a meal, Frethirik shared our encounter with the crew. The firelight flickered on his face, casting a warm, orange light on the hard lines and bruises that told the story of our survival. At that moment, we all sat united, Jan's entire band of warriors, bonded closely by the battles we had overcome over the past few weeks.

When Frethirik finished, everyone sat staring into the fire. I took a bite of salted pork. 'So anyone know why these men attacked us? We only just arrived, immediately ambushed by these robbers. Is that a common occurrence in this country?'

'Probably came from Ipswich.' Trollmann, of course, knew the answer to the mystery. 'Thralls escaped their masters in these parts. We heard of a famine a few weeks back. Many starved due to a bad harvest. It always brings about chaos, hitting those poorest the most. That is why these enslaved souls escaped into the woods. At least there they can hunt, and enjoy a sense of freedom.'

'Yeah, hunt traders passing by,' Jan grunted, his brows knitting. 'No matter how hard they got hit, a thrall must just accept his fate, not rob others of their life and coin.'

The group reflected on the situation in silence, the air crisp and still, a quiet tension hanging over the camp like a heavy blanket. In the distance, the first glimmers of light appeared on the horizon as a faint rosy hue spread across the sky. The sunrise cast long, slanting rays of golden light over the landscape, illuminating our weary faces and filling the camp with a hopeful glow. The light touched the dew drops on the grass, turning them into shimmering jewels, while the distant hills were painted purple and pink. My weariness was energized by chirping birds and rustling leaves in the cool breeze as nature awoke to a new day.

After a prayer and a silent breakfast, Jan decided we better move on. 'Who knows how many more thralls escaped from Ipswich? I do not feel like taking on twenty more hungry bandits. Let's pack up and head to town. The light now allows for safe passage so it won't take long to reach Ipswich.'

We sailed up the river, taking in the new landscape now clearly visible. Strangely, it looked very similar to Frisia along this river. Traveling inland, we passed lush fields abundant with sheep and cows. Patches of woodland dotted the countryside, and the distant call of an owl or woodpecker echoed through the trees. A tranquil, peaceful place in contrast to the recent violence. But that was our world, a paradise one moment and chaos the next, a constant battle between order and disorder, light and darkness, life and death. And while the beauty of the world could not be denied, the struggles of survival always tempered it.

It did not take long to reach Ipswich. I only counted some three villages we passed before the town came into view, surrounded by a wooden palisade and reinforced by towers and gates, much like Thuredrith at home. As we drew closer, we spotted its busy docks, where ships of all shapes and sizes unloaded their cargoes of wool, timber, and other goods. The sounds and smells of the town wafted over the river, the clanging of blacksmiths' hammers, dogs barking, and ships in repair. Nearing the wharves to dock our snekkja, Frethirik counted twenty vessels moored there. Their decks bustled with sailors, labourors, and merchants. The air now thickened with the sour tang of the town.

The quayside breathed a hive of activity, with merchants and their assistants bustling to and fro, loading and unloading goods. Barrels of ale and wine rolled along the dock, with sacks of grain and flour hoisted onto waiting carts. As we docked, a middle-aged man with a grey beard approached to greet Jan, who clearly knew him. They shook hands, Jan handing over some silver to the townsman. They mumbled to each other, our captain pointing towards the sea. The greybeard frowned, then nodded his head ferociously. He clapped Jan on the shoulders and sent a boy into town.

When Jan came back, he ordered Rurik to oversee the unloading of the cog while waving Trollmann, Robert, Frethirik, and me over to him. Jan wore his usual smile again. 'All right fellows, I know we're all tired and need rest, but I just spoke to the harbourmaster, who invited me to Ipswich's hall to speak to Thegn Ralf, the lord of Ipswich. He desires to hear your story of the robbers. Oh, and Reginhard, the harbourmaster also mentioned two monks who arrived three days ago. They said they came from Echternach.'

I glanced at Robert, who raised his brows, shaking his head. So they got here before us, just as we expected. Damn, they could already be heading to the location of the ring.

Jan now led us into town. 'Apparently they left towards

London yesterday. But the thegn can tell you more, I'm sure. We do some odd jobs for him at times, so I know him quite well. I'm sure he's willing to tell you what transpired with the monks after you share your story with him. Now let's go see him.'

We trudged through the streets of Ipswich, our feet so burdened with fatigue that we hardly made it through the market street. Even though weariness struck my bones, it still fascinated me how many stalls displayed pottery there. Trollmann explained that Frisians settled in Ipswich centuries ago, setting up a pottery trade that still survived.

The pottery vendors sold their wares along the edge of the market street, displaying an array of beautifully crafted vessels and dishes. I gaped at jugs, bowls, platters, and plates of all shapes and sizes, each carefully crafted and decorated with intricate designs. Floral patterns adorned some, while others featured Christian shapes and symbols. Even though Jan urged us on, I couldn't help but stop at one stall and feel the rough texture of the earthenware, running my hands over it. But then Frethirik pushed me on, shaking his head at the vendor who named his price.

Despite our lack of sleep, the vibrant energy of the market drew us in, with its colourful array of goods on display, until we stood in front of the thegn's hall, placed on a mound just outside of the market. It had a thatched roof, and its long and narrow shape was reminiscent of the hall in Starum. But unlike that hall, Ralf's was at least twice the size and was surrounded by a wall. The wooden palisade, sturdy wooden stakes, were sharpened at the top to deter any would-be intruders. We stopped in front of its gate, guarded by several armed men.

They recognised Jan, welcoming us to move on. Laughter and music came from the hall, and once inside, the smell of roasting meat greeted us. Smoke rose from the open hearth in the hall's centre where Thegn Ralf sat in a plush, richly decorated chair. The nobleman's belly protruded from his fine woolen tunic, and his face, red and sweaty, was decorated with a large, black moustache.

The warmth of the fire welcomed us as our tired eyes steadily adjusted to the dim light. The interior of the hall, as impressive as the exterior, showed walls decorated with banners, shields, and various weapons. Frethirik smirked at me. 'Well, he must be comfortable.'

Lord Ralph looked up as we entered. A group of men surrounded him, all dressed in similar finery, drinking from silver goblets, their jovial conversation filling the air. Despite his girth, Ralf rose easily from his seat and strode over to greet us. He extended a meaty hand, his grip firm and strong. 'Welcome, travelers,' he boomed. 'I am Thegn Ralf, and this is my hall. Please, join us and partake of our hospitality.'

I struggled to understand his words as I stepped forward to greet him, as it was the first time I had heard English spoken. But despite the language barrier, I managed to follow his gestures and tone of voice, grateful for his warm welcome.

Thegn Ralf led us to a table near the fire, signaling to his servants, who quickly brought platters of food and jugs of ale. My belly rumbling again, I felt glad that the food smelled of the highest quality, with roasted meats, stews, and breads all on offer, almost as if there had been no famine at all. We settled in to enjoy the hospitality of the lord and his men, our fatigue and hunger forgotten for the moment.

The ale tasted rich and flavourful, flowing freely throughout the hall. After we had taken our first sip, the thegn addressed us properly, a deep frown covering his face. 'I heard bandits troubled you on your way here. Alas, something that happens more often to travelers since our thralls escaped in the spring.'

As Ralf spoke, I focused intently on his words, surprised that I understood him well enough. While I had never spoken English before, its similarity to my native Frisian made me grasp the meaning of his words.

Jan nodded at me, allowing me to speak. 'It is true Lord Ralf, that we got attacked by bandits. We defeated them though.'

The thegn shook his head, his eyes closed for a moment. When he opened them again, he reached into his tunic, fumbling for something. He threw a silver penny on the table, grinning. 'Okay so I hope that some of your men can assist me with a little problem here Jan. Your son and his companion seem capable enough. If they wish to join our posse in the afternoon, I welcome them.'

He pointed at the coin. 'Five of these for every thrall you kill.' He threw me and Frethirik a bag of silver. 'That's a start since you took care of some of them.'

Robert beamed when he saw the coin. 'Lord, I too will join. I train that little brat over there, and brought my destrier across the sea.' Thegn Ralf, beaming at the scarred Norman, now clapped his hands. 'Great, more warriors to join our posse. Oh but one more thing fellows. Their leader is a special case. Ever heard of the name Grendel?'

I shook my head, much to the surprise of the courtiers, who mumbled at each other, their eyes widening. Ralf sighed. 'Of course, you are foreign and do not know our tales, our heroes or our monsters. See, Grendel was a great villain who plagued the Danes in the legend of Beowulf. Now Ipswich has a similar problem – the bandits – and so we call their leader Grendel.'

Thegn Ralf's face twitched. 'Already single-handedly killed

ten of my warriors. Ten!' He slammed his fist on the table. 'Our community, as well as a good number of traders, bear much pain because of these thralls. So justice must prevail.' He raised his finger, the hall now silent. His voice turned a whisper as if the bandits could overhear us somehow. 'If you kill this Grendel I'll pay you thirty pennies.'

Robert, almost choking on his ale, nodded ferociously at the proposal. 'Of course, we accept Lord Ralf. We will chase these criminals for you.' He slowly stood up to raise his goblet at the whole assembly. 'Death to the rebels.'

All courtiers raised their goblets as a chorus of hatred rang throughout the hall. Grendel better be prepared for this because he won't survive if we find him.

Chapter Fifteen

As we trudged to one of the inns that adorned Ipswich, my mind kept wondering. 'Why did they escape their duties only to become outlaws?' I just couldn't wrap my head around it.

Trollmann lifted his eyebrows in his habitual, vexing manner, causing his eyes to appear unnaturally large. 'What would you do if your children died from starvation?'

I admitted that made sense. 'But why does the rest of the town not look famished then?'

'Trade, Reginhard. Trade and fishing. It is the countryside that gets hit first. The thralls work the land and hand over a portion of their food to their master, just like the peasants did in Veenkoop. Only when there is nothing to harvest they get nothing for themselves. This while most townspeople are still able to buy supplies through trade. It is one of the harsh realities of our world, lad.'

I frowned, realising the English thralls were even worse off than our Frisian peasants, who seemed to enjoy a bit more freedom in the newly cleared colonies. 'So Trollmann, who is this Beowulf anyway? And that Grendel, what was that about?'

The Sami's eyes sparkled. 'Well, you see, Beowulf was a great warrior and leader in battle, who had to face the demon Grendel, a hairy and massive troll, as ancient as the earth itself.' He made a throat-slitting gesture. 'Beowulf killed Grendel of course, as you will the thrall leader.'

'We'll see about that then. Will you actually join Robert and me with the posse, Trollmann?'

'No, you are on your own lad. Jan told me we depart on another mission. It seems Thegn Ralf fears some Danish pirates snooping around, which we are to take on. I think this evening might be the last for us together.'

My heart sank at my friend's words, a deep sadness welling up inside me. We had just reunited. Yet my own sense of purpose equally filled me with excitement as Robert and I would finally fight together and maybe even earn some silver. I had never earned anything before, so the thought was thrilling. I clutched the sack of coins Frethirik and I had split – seven pennies already; think of the ale I could buy.

When we arrived at the inn, we immediately noticed the large copper bell hanging from the door, which bore the name of the establishment, 'The Copper Bell.' Grateful to find a place to rest, we relaxed before the landlord woke us from our slumber.

'Frisian sirs, there are a posse of guardsmen waiting outside for you.'

Robert jumped up, grumbling for me to follow suit. We helped each other into our mail hauberks and stepped outside. Once there, we got stared down by a group of ten guardsmen dressed in practical but unadorned woolen garb, some sporting leather tabards over their tunics. The guards carried various weapons, including axes, clubs, and spears, which glinted in the faint light of the cloudy afternoon. A ragtag group, but with a stern demeanor, they stood in silent formation, their eyes fixated on us. The air charged with suspicion as they took us in, their eyes not even blinking once.

Eventually, a man dressed in the plainest leather tabard extended his hand in invitation. Robert and I approached cautiously, then we shook his hand. To my surprise, the men's faces almost immediately broke into faint smiles. One of the guards even tossed an alesack to a companion, causing a ripple of laughter to spread through the group. It was as if a spell had been broken as we suddenly stood among newfound comrades, united by the simple pleasures of drink and camaraderie.

Their leader introduced himself as Einar, a Dane just like Thegn Ralf. He then pointed at each guardsman, grunting each man's name in a mixed accent of Saxon and Dane. They then mounted their stocky palfreys, which looked like simple farm animals and workhorses unsuitable for warfare. But, better that than walking, I thought.

The moment Gerold handed us the reins, Einar took the lead, our posse setting out towards the northeast. We rode through some fields and past a small community before arriving at a vast expanse of thick, muddy marshland – a treacherous, unforgiving terrain with reeds and brackish water stretching as far as the eye could see. A perfect place for rebels to hide out, I thought. The horses picked their way carefully through the marsh, their hooves squelching in the mud as we struggled to keep our balance. The landscape felt so desolate and haunting, with an isolation that sent a chill down my spine.

'Quite like home, isn't it Robert?' I asked my usually quiet companion.

He grimaced. 'Bloody marches. Hate them. Can't ride down infantry without getting stuck.'

That woke up our leader, who had stayed equally silent throughout the march. 'You're right enough Frank. That is why we fight in shield walls without bloody horses. Only get in the way, them things.' He spat. 'Still, these bandit bastards dress lightly and are quick on their feet too. What's more, they know the terrain as well as I do. So be on the lookout, Frisian friends. Their arrows sting.'

'I'm no bloody Frisian,' Robert grumbled at me when Einar was out of earshot again. 'Nor a snorting Frank!'

I laughed. 'Won't make the same mistake as the Germans anyway, will we, Robert? Some years ago, they tried to kill Count Dirk of Holland. He lured them into the marsh and waited for their cavalry to charge. They did exactly that but got stuck in the mud. It became a complete massacre the Germans still haven't forgotten about.' I shrugged, flicking my eyes towards shadows cast by the willow trees around us, my story hitting the reality of our position in the bud. The Germans had been ambushed in an eerily similar landscape.

A while later, after having rested for a bit, we headed into a forest. With another ale in our bellies, Einar cheered up significantly, now spouting jokes to his men.

'We must be nearing their den.' He suddenly pointed at an insignificant slope. 'A woodcutter told me he saw a group of outlaws around here. I think they could be up there. It has always been a favourite hiding place for outlaws.' He grinned. 'Most likely, they've got some wenches with them too.' Einar rubbed his hands. 'A good number of women escaped with the male thralls.'

His remark surprised me, as I only expected to face young men. My mind raced back to Ragnar slaying my village, with Gerda dying in agony after his rotten Vikings had done God knows what with her. I got triggered by the memory, Einar's boorish tongue making my blood boil. 'Damn barbarian,' I whispered to Robert. 'I thought these English were Christian folk.'

Einar raised his alesack. 'Of course, since they're all outlawed we can do with 'm as we please, hahaha!' That remark caused much laughter from the guards, another sack of ale passing around the merry band. Einar glanced at me, grinning widely. 'Guess what I'm talkin' about now heh. Listen to the riddle and try to guess what I am.'

I nodded wearily.

'I travel on foot, trampling the earth underneath me – the fields, the marshes, and the sands – as long as I carry a spirit,' Einar declared, his voice tinged with bravado. 'And if I die, I bind fast dark Welshmen, sometimes even better men!' He chuckled. 'Get it?'

I shook my head, no idea what he was on about. Weird sense of humour these English had.

Einar just continued his strange joke, clearly oblivious to my increasing discomfort. 'Sometimes,' he went on, 'I give a brave warrior a drink from my belly, while sometimes a very noble bride places her foot on me; sometimes a dark Celtic slave from Wales shakes me and presses me to her, while sometimes a dumb drunk maid in the dark of the night wets me with water while she warms for a while by the pleasant fireplace. On my chest she places a hand and rubs it often, after which I see nothing but darkness. Can you guess what I am, that living, ravages the land and after I die serves . . . .'

Before Einar could finish his sentence, the horses in the front row started staggering, their riders screaming out. 'Watch out. We're attacked!' Black pointy shadows rained down on them, and one of the guards fell from his horse, an arrow lodged in his throat. Einar shook his head, shouting orders at everyone to dismount. 'Raise your shields, men.' We immediately sprang into action, drawing our weapons. Before I knew it, our battle had begun.

'Shieldwall! Shieldwall!'

As arrows rained at us from all directions, Robert's horse got bogged down in the mud, and he fell off. Despite this setback, the rest of us safely reached Einar to form a small block of men, two lines strong. The back line then used their shields to cover the heads of the first line, while the men in front, Einar and me in the centre, used our shields to cover the rest of our body.

I glanced at Robert. He seemed all right, now slowly getting up with a raised shield. 'Wait, men!' Einar commanded, a breeze cooling the air around us. Bated breaths surrounded me, some men whispering, 'Keep your shield up,' their eyes wide as they scanned the forest. 'Brunwulf, can you see them?' Einar inquired from one of the men.

After gazing at the hills for a while, this Brunwulf pointed east. 'There they are, master. Up that hill yonder.' I followed the guard's finger, seeing ten brigands at the top of a nearby hill. They looked fully prepared for a fight, armed with simple clubs, axes, and bows.

I inhaled slowly, trying to calm my nerves, my heart thumping. My mouth was dry, and my palms felt sweaty. The rush of battle began to course through my veins, and I knew I had to stay focused to survive.

'Alright, let's move forward. Slowly, men,' Einar commanded, his voice steady despite our tactical disadvantage. 'Reginhard, listen lad, you have another job. You and Robert take your horses and try to flank the bastards. Look at the hill, see how you can approach them from the west, where there is little foliage to block your path?' He pointed at the trees. 'If we surprise them from two sides, we can easily cut them down. You just have to follow the river, the trees blocking you from view, until your reach that side of the hill.' Einar clapped my back. 'Watch out for their arrows, though. They sting even you warriors wrapped in iron!'

Nodding, I rushed back to Winney, grabbed her reins and

then charged towards Robert with my shield raised high. 'Bloody hell,' the Norman veteran groaned as I checked on him. 'I am getting old, lad.' Despite his complaints, my mentor jumped on his horse as athletically as a teenager.

'And fat,' I jested. 'Took you all this time just to get back on your feet. Now let's go, greybeard, Einar has a plan!'

I led us to the trees, storming through the bushes to make a wide circle possible, hoping the bandits had all their focus on Einar's approach. This would only work if we could surprise them utterly. We couldn't see the bandits anymore, but I knew we had to follow that river until the hill came into view again.

'That slope isn't very high, is it?' I shouted at Robert. 'We can hit the enemy hard on their flank. That will allow Einar to storm into their band to finish them,' I reasoned. 'But we have to wait until the guards are far enough up the slope to assist us. We cannot just charge them blindly. First we hide in the nearest bush, then we strike at the right time.'

Robert nodded his approval, beaming at me. 'You're quite the weasel my young friend. Your father's reputation precedes you.'

After thundering through the woods, I smiled when I spotted the bandits up the slope, just as Einar had assured me. Yet now we had to be careful they didn't see us in turn. We stormed to the bushes at the foot of the slope and dismounted to wait for Einar's advance. Fortunately, the guards were marching up the hill, blocking arrows throughout their steady ascent. I admitted I was impressed. My training allowed me to assess the quality of these troops, and even though the posse was just a militia, they were well led and disciplined. Einar was a man to be respected, his leadership outshining his earlier boorishness.

After the guards finally marched halfway up, Robert grumbled at me. 'Now lad, finally we put that training to use!' We charged out as fast as we could, our swords unsheathed. As we thundered up the slope, the bandits turned, their eyes bulging out of their sockets. We didn't even give them a chance to react, closing in on them from horseback, the element of surprise and the height of our animals a deadly advantage. I swung my sword down, connecting with one of the bandit's leather tabards, knocking him off his feet. Robert's blade caught another one on the shoulder, and he fell to the ground, groaning.

The other thralls scrambled to their feet, trying to fight, but they were no match for trained horsemen. We hacked at them, our swords clanging against their spears and clubs. One swung his axe at me, but I dodged it, my weapon finding its mark on his chest. Another tried to spear Robert, who parried the blow, slicing through the bandit's leather armor.

The two remaining bandits started running away with us in pursuit. We caught up with them quickly, roaring for their surrender. They just dropped their weapons, raising their hands in defeat. Robert tied their hands together, and we led them back to our group.

The posse had already taken care of the wounded bandits, their heads now hung low. The rest of our men cheered as they saw us return with the captured bandits. Yet, we couldn't rest as Brunwulf pointed at two more thralls fleeing down the slope.

After handing my prisoner to Einar, I swirled around, going after them. Robert followed a few feet behind until we saw the bandits split ways. I pointed left, ready to chase that one, and I heard Robert grunt his approval as he moved to the right.

Gaining speed, I yelled at the wretch to surrender, but he ran straight into dense woods. Before I knew it, he danced into foliage so thick I could no longer chase him on horseback. I reluctantly dismounted to continue on foot, dragging Winney by the reins. 'Stop, you bugger.' Didn't help, of course – the bugger didn't stop.

He looked back, a shadowy face under a hooded brown cloth, even his mouth covered. Determined to catch the bastard, I kept hacking through the branches and bushes on my path. I had to work hard as my mail shirt slowed me down considerably.

Out of nowhere, several sharp blows slammed into my chest, knocking the air out of my lungs and sending me crashing to the forest floor. Breathless, I tried to rise, but the weight of my mail made it too difficult. I gritted my teeth, feeling the pain of the arrows that had hit my armour. Blast it; I have to survive this, I thought, as I crawled towards the nearest tree for cover.

My vision blurred, the forest spinning around me. I struggled to regain my senses, the pain in my chest unbearable, each breath challenging. I pushed myself to a stand, but my legs gave way under me.

Completely defenseless, I was at the mercy of my attackers. Blasted ambush, I thought, thinking back on the story of the Germans. How could I have been so careless? Was I not a Frisian, of the race that claimed to be experts in guerrilla warfare?

As I lay there, a hooded figure stepped out from behind a tree, followed by two more bandits armed with bows. They glared at me from a safe distance, their twisted smiles taunting me. The one I chased addressed me in a high-pitched voice. 'You should have stayed in your town,' he sneered. 'Now you will suffer the same fate as those before you.'

I tried to talk, anything to defend myself, but the pain of each breath was excruciating. All I could do was stare up at him, my eyes pleading for mercy. There was none to be found in his cold gaze. I couldn't let them kill me, and wincing, I tried to regain my breath. Slowly, steadily, I stood, raising my sword to defy these criminals. I refused to give up, refused to die.

The two hooded companions grunted, each nocking another arrow to finish me. I knew my mail could take another blow, their bows not nearly as strong as our crossbows. Survival was all that counted. The bandits loosed their arrows, and I dodged to the right, one swooping past my arm and another hitting the tree I just leaned on. This is it, I thought. I just had to charge as fast as I could now.

Roaring defiantly, I raced towards my attackers, ready to take them down before they could nock another arrow. The first man dropped his bow, trying to unsheathe a dagger, but he was already too late. I swiftly sliced through the brigand's chest. He let out a blood-curdling scream as he collapsed to the ground, his efforts to stem the bleeding in vain. As the second man raised a hatchet to strike me, I used my longer sword to hack open his knees. He began to fall, and I plunged my sword into his heart before he could utter a sound. I witnessed his soul leave his body before he even hit the ground.

I then chased my last target into the forest. Though winded by all the effort, I prepared to dispatch my last foe. 'No one left now. Better if you surrender and follow me willingly,' I demanded, raising my sword. 'Now show yourself, bandit!'

He didn't oppose me or make any move to flee. Instead, he simply removed the hood and cloth covering his mouth. In shock, I faltered. Rather than a ragged bandit, I gazed at the face of a young woman. Her dark hair fell in wild waves around her face, framing her thin, delicate features. Despite the appearance of fragility, a particular strength emanated from her intense gaze, demanding respect.

Her striking green eyes pierced straight through mine, holding me completely immobile. Her long, subtle nose accentuated the sharpness of her glare, adding to the mystique of her stunning features. She had an air of mystery, leaving me with an overwhelming desire to know more about her story. Yet despite her captivating beauty, I also sensed a deep sorrow in her eyes, hinting at a more complex inner world that lay just beyond the surface.

Chapter Sixteen

'I know what they told you,' the green-eyed girl started in a strange accent of English, one I hadn't heard before in Ipswich. She looked at her fallen comrades, her face fixed on the deadly scene for a while, unblinking, unyielding. Though her companions were no longer with her, she somehow refused to avert her gaze as if to imprint their memory upon her mind. Yet despite her sudden loss, her stoic expression betrayed no emotion, her face hard as stone. What would she have gone through, I thought, her whole appearance raising so many questions.

Unwavering, she faced me again, her words departing her lips as calmly as if she stood in the market, buying groceries. 'Since you have not killed me yet, tell me something, young man. Your armour reveals you are a warrior, not part of the guard from Ipswich. So, who are you?'

Even though I was the one who should be asking the questions, my sword at her throat, I felt compelled to reply. I explained the details of Thegn Ralf's orders, and she listened intently, her eyes neutral and unemotional, almost as if she had already anticipated the worst and was now simply resigned to her fate. Despite my nervousness, her calm demeanor had a strangely soothing effect on me, and I found myself speaking more freely and openly than I had initially intended.

Once I finished recounting everything I knew, a moment of contemplation silenced us both. I could hear the faint sound of a stream rushing by and the distant chirping of birds in the woods beyond. The young woman's gaze remained steady, and I felt unsure of what to say or do.

Finally, she spoke. 'Thank you for telling me all of this,' she said, her voice barely above a whisper. 'I knew there was a reason we were attacked, but I had no idea that Thegn Ralf wanted us dead so badly.' Her eyes misted with anger. 'We simply starved in our hovels and saw no other option than to leave our village. Just twenty men, eight women, and six children survived to venture out into the wilds. Some came from Saxon lands, their families in debt, others, like me, slaves from Ireland. We want nothing more than to survive and if possible to taste the freedom we once enjoyed.'

I understood her wish but felt helpless. 'I cannot guarantee that Thegn Ralf will leave you alone, but I assure you that I have no intention of harming anyone else here. My only goal is to complete our task, to eliminate the threat of the rebels.'

I paused for a moment, considering my words. 'I can tell the guards that these two enemies were the last of your group. Commander Einar will want to return to Ipswich before nightfall, which means you will have the opportunity to escape from this place. I suggest you leave as soon as possible, as he may return to search this area another day.'

She concurred, her eyes still fixed on mine. 'I believe you,' she whispered, her tone softening slightly. 'I know you're just doing what you've been told to do. These are dangerous times, and it's easy to get caught up in violence and bloodshed. We unwillingly are anyway.'

That struck a chord, and my admiration for this woman was complete. Despite her hardships and losses, she remained strong and resilient, a true survivor in a world that seemed to be constantly tearing itself apart around her. I grew fascinated by her, unwilling to leave her side, but equally aware I had to return to Ipswich soon. What was I to do with her?

She sighed, finally breaking the spell of her gaze as she closed her eyes, the wind blowing her hair wildly around her.

'Please follow me warrior, it will only take a moment. We are close. I just want you to see what conditions the English force their thralls to live in before you leave again. At the very least I will have gained a small victory this day, spreading some awareness. At least God will witness some good came out of this bloody day.'

She paused, her intense green eyes piercing mine again. 'But if you betray me at least end our suffering quickly. Do not capture us and bring us to Ipswich in chains. I know our fate is sealed this day, with all our men now dead. I do not see how it still matters anyway.'

Strangely, I found myself unable to refuse her request. Something in her words sounded sincere, and I felt a strange connection to her and her struggles. Her declaration reminded me of Ragnar's attack on my village, and a wave of guilt washed over me. What had we done to this woman and her people? In their eyes, we were like Ragnar, and the weight of my own actions now hit home. This was not the glorious battle I had imagined. Instead, the harsh reality of war and the cost of our attack sobered me straight up. I had killed no other than poor souls, starving wretches who fought hard to survive each day. May God forgive me.

As we walked, the woman's steps, though measured and calm, held a certain resignation. Her eyes remained focused on the path ahead despite the tears that now glistened on her cheeks, breaking my guilty soul even more. I followed her in silence, contemplating the cruel realities of war.

We approached a small clearing in the forest, the woman

pointing ahead to a collection of crude huts made of sticks and mud. A makeshift fence made of wooden stakes surrounded the clearing. I could see a group of people huddled inside, their faces drained, their eyes wearied with desperation.

The woman stepped up to the fence and called out in a language I didn't understand. An old man approached cautiously, looking at us suspiciously, but the woman reassured him in a low, urgent tone. Finally, the man nodded in agreement, opening the shabby gate to let us in.

The scene wrenched at my heart as malnourished and exhausted children, covered with bruises and cuts, huddled together under a makeshift roof. The overwhelming stench of feces and urine filled my nostrils, the lack of basic hygiene evident. The woman walked straight to another old man who sat huddled in a corner, and she took his hand in hers. She spoke to him softly, in that language I didn't understand, and he nodded, his eyes beaming with gratitude.

I felt a lump in my throat as I took in these people's horrible living conditions. A stark reminder of the brutality of life, where the innocent are often shattered in its wake.

Feeling at a loss for words, I sat between the woman and the elderly man, unable to utter useless words or meaningless sounds. None would help these thralls, these wretches. God, it would be an act of mercy to just finish them off with my sword.

After a while, I couldn't take it anymore, finally blurting out what tugged at my heart. 'The wretches are famished.' Somehow, this made me go back in time to the death of my family. I never heard of any survivors from Veenkoop. Did any survive aside from Gerold? Did Ragnar enslave some of them, only for them to end up like this? Hell, could they even have ended up here? Had I killed some of my own villagers?

My remark produced a frown on the woman's pale face. 'It is not easy for us. They took most of us as slaves and sold us in Dublin. There was a raid on my village and they . . . they took me. They did horrible things, those bastards.'

She sighed, her fatigue visible on her mud-covered face. 'They stripped me naked and sold me to the highest bidder, who then took most of us here to Ipswich, where that dog Ralf became our master.' She spit on the floor in disdain.

I felt so sorry now I had joined Ralf's guards. All of this proved so unfair, so utterly cruel, so much like what had been done to me by Count Floris.

She moved on to an old woman who was weak from a wracking cough, and handed the sick woman some herbs to chew. I wondered if it would help at all.

'After a cattle famine last year we just fled here, trying to survive. But now that we're also outlawed it's becoming impossible. They chase us everywhere.'

I could not answer to such cruelty, so nodded with understanding, again realising I was in a serious predicament. Looking at this miserable lot, I knew Ralf would probably kill most of these thralls since they had rebelled against him. While I couldn't rat them out, I also had no idea how to help them.

'We certainly aren't this harsh in Frisia. Our villagers have a lot more freedom than the thralls here.'

'Sounds like quite the paradise.'

'Well until some count took my lands and murdered everyone. So I know a little of how you feel, I guess.' I jumped up in frustration. 'Look, I will try to help you, but these poor beggars . . . well there's not much I can do.'

I considered the situation for a moment. 'Keep hidden here,

and then come for me at night. Go to the big rock near Ipswich, which should be far enough from any guards. I will tell them I killed the two bandits but couldn't find any more.'

The woman didn't look convinced. 'And why would you be doing this?'

'For one, you seem very good with a bow, as I still feel the bruises.' I touched the parts where the arrows had hit my mail coat. Then I realised that was no answer to her question at all. 'And second . . . .' I felt my face turn red. 'Well, never mind, just go there.'

An amused expression crossed her face, but she seemed to accept my unclear, improvisational plan. 'All right then, I'll have to trust you.' Again, her penetrating eyes bore into mine. 'I seem to have no choice, and I trust the look in your eyes, as you have not harmed us yet. I believe your claim to have been similarly mistreated as myself.' Her frown darkened before she continued, 'yet I warn you I will slit your throat if you betray me. I won't appear unless I see no one but you near that rock.'

Looking toward the sun, I realised I had already spent too much time here, as the posse must be wondering where I was.

About to move away, I glanced back one more time. 'I am Reginhard by the way.'

Her piercing green eyes, which had until now seemed so cold and unyielding, suddenly took on a warm, glowing quality that I had never before encountered in a woman. Her hand moved to her chest.

'Ciara.'

I smiled, delighted to discover her name, relieved she accepted me. Then, forcing myself from her eyes, I nodded curtly and left. I really hoped she would come to Ipswich. God in Heaven, I prayed my plan would work. I truly wanted to rescue her from this fate, to save them all.

What a woman, an angel, so different from Veenkoop's girls. Wilder than a Frisian ministerial's daughter, yet vastly more eloquent than a peasant and much more refined in speech, even in a language originally not her own. She even led an entire band of men; in truth, she utterly impressed me.

Chapter Seventeen

After our conversation's somewhat awkward but satisfactory end, I returned to the dead thralls, finding Winney. She grazed calmly, neighing softly when she saw me approach. I took a moment to stroke her mane, feeling her warm breath on my hand. She nuzzled my arm affectionately as if sensing my unease. I took a deep breath and tried to clear my mind, taking in the peaceful scene of the sun still high in the sky, where, visible through a gap in the trees, it was shining over some hills in the distance.

I threw the bodies onto Winney's back and traced my steps back to the posse, where Robert and Einar hovered over a dozen dead bodies. Our group seemed okay, with only four wounded by the arrows that had slipped through the shield wall.

'Well'? Einar growled at me. 'Did you manage to capture another one?' I tapped the bodies on the horse. 'Two even.' Robert grinned at me. 'That's seventy pennies in total.'

Einar smiled too. He took a sack of ale from a dead body, taking a deep sip. 'Not a bad result here.' He held up the ale in front of him, frowning. 'They must have stolen this.' He threw the ale to Robert, who grunted thanks, emptying it in one go. Einar then jumped on his horse. 'Frisians! Let us get back and report to Thegn Ralf. I am sure he'll be pleased. We will split the rewards, sounds fair, right?'

For a moment, Robert seemed about to object, his grin melting away into a grimace. But then he just shrugged. Even though we had killed more thralls, Einar's suggestion was quite fair, as both groups had done their duty, with equal danger to their lives.

Once back in Ipswich, Thegn Ralf hosted a fine dinner at his hall. He thanked us for our service, even offering Robert and me a spot at his table that night. Mead and ale flowed freely, with a bounty of roasted meats and vegetables on the table. The hall filled with laughter and merriment as Thegn Ralf and his warriors celebrated their victory over the thralls. During the feast, the lord regaled us with stories of past battles and heroic deeds, his voice booming across the room.

But all the while, my thoughts kept wandering to the thralls left in misery, my mood as dark as the ale in my cup. Even when Thegn Ralf threw Robert and me a bag of well-earned silver, the sour taste in my mouth wouldn't leave me. After dinner, I departed with the excuse of needing sleep. Yet my plan, now hatched to completion, took me on a different path. I trudged to the harbour to affect my solution to Ciara's troubles, then headed to the rock we passed earlier, well outside the town's periphery.

The full moon illuminated the dirt path, casting a silvery glow over the landscape as I slipped out of town. As I rode, a rocky outcropping on the horizon gradually came into view. The only sound in the cool night air was that of horse hooves crunching along the dirt road. As I drew closer to the rock, I could see its rough surface reflecting the moonlight, casting strange shadows around its base. Yet no Ciara.

Dismounting, I cast my eyes around. Did she decide not to come? 'Please show yourself, Ciara,' I mumbled, hoping she hadn't stayed in their hideout. I then felt a sharp object in my back, and from both sides of the rock, two shadowy figures appeared, arrows pointing at me. A voice behind me hissed into my ear. 'Are you truly on your own, Reginhard?' Recognising her voice, that was definitely Ciara, I thought.

I nodded slowly, my breath shallow. The figures stepped out of the shadows, revealing themselves as two young women, each with a wild look in their eyes. I swallowed hard, feeling the cold steel of the dagger against my back. 'I was only hired by Thegn Ralf to hunt down a band of thralls,' I replied, trying to keep my voice steady. 'I have no other business with him or anyone else in this town anymore.'

The two women exchanged a quick glance, and the smallest one lowered her bow slightly. 'Prove it,' she hissed. 'Empty your pockets.' I slowly turned around, my hands raised in surrender. I knew I had nothing to hide, but the thought of these two women going through my belongings made me uneasy. Nonetheless, I emptied my pockets, revealing three pieces of bread, a dagger, and a parchment with Bishop William's seal.

The women scrutinised each item carefully, examining them one by one. After a few moments, they nodded at each other. 'Seems like he's telling the truth,' the smaller one said, throwing her companion a loaf of bread. 'But we'll be keeping an eye on you.'

Ciara sheathed the dagger. The other women lowered their bows, and then all three tore into the bread. They ate in silence, the only sound the rustle of bread and an occasional slurp of water.

After finishing her meal, Ciara turned back towards me. 'So, what brings you to meet me out here. What is it you want from me?' Her high voice sounded welcoming, but her eyes darted back and forth. Clearly, she didn't trust me yet, so I would need to earn her confidence before she would fully open up to me.

'As I told you before, I suffered a horrible fate at my own village not so long ago. I saw how your people suffered in the camp, and I realised we have just added to your misery by killing the men that supported your group. For all this pain we inflicted I wanted to help you, not only to clear my own conscience, but because I believe in my own fate. I believe God wants me to help you out of this situation, and it is what I believe my father would have done.'

Ciara raised an eyebrow. 'Even if I believe you, what could you possibly do for us? I would say you already did enough by killing half our group.'

I shrugged. 'Look it may sound strange, but I have found a way to help you. I belong to the tribe of Frisians, and I come from across the sea. I traveled with a group of settlers who are to clear some land here for the Bishop of Elmham. It seems all this is part of a deal made by my own lord, the Bishop of Wiltenburg. In return, the English bishop agreed to help me obtain a sacred relic connected to our town.'

Ciara's two companions exchanged glances with her, the small one arching one eyebrow. 'Well, even if that may be, how does that help us?'

Taking a sip of water, I chose my next words carefully. 'I earned some silver by taking on your group. Instead of putting it in my pocket, I decided to hand it over to the headman of the Frisian settlers.' I stepped closer to Ciara, placing my hands on her shoulders. 'I made a deal he would take in your group, no questions asked. Of course I promised you would all participate in the newfound colony, but I made him swear he would keep everything between us. Thegn Ralf will never know, and for all everyone cares your group simply disappeared. Kill two birds with one stone I believe the English say.'

The women now stepped away, mumbling among themselves for a bit, Ciara pointing frantically at me now and then. Finally, she convinced the others, walking over to me, penetrating my eyes in that overwhelming fashion again.

I stood nailed to the ground, praying they would accept. At least I would have done something good in my life. At least I would have saved their group, something I couldn't do with Veenkoop. As she approached, I felt uneasy under her intense gaze. She stopped in front of me, her eyes still locked onto mine. For a moment, she said nothing, just scanning my face as if to read my thoughts. Finally, she nodded. 'Somehow, I trust you Reginhard. My group simply has no future left so it seems it is all we can do anyway. We hardly have a choice, and I know that if you wanted to betray us you could have done so already, and we would now be dead.'

Ciara's voice deepened as she spoke. There was a weariness in her voice as if she had carried the burden of her people's struggles for a long time. Too long. I nodded, feeling a pang of respect for her and her group. 'I understand,' I said, my tone hushed. 'I'll do my best to give them a chance at a better life.'

She gave me a small, sad smile before turning towards her companions. 'We leave to make arrangements,' she announced. Then she faced me again, eyes scanning mine for any detail they may have missed. Trust was hard to come by if you experienced what she had, I thought, my heart bleeding. Especially when you stand before the killer of your friends, who promises to save what's left of them. What would I have done if Count Floris had said that to me?

'I hope you understand, Reginhard, that I'm only doing this because I have no other choice,' Ciara said, her voice low. 'I don't trust anyone, especially not someone who collaborates with those who enslaved and killed our people.'

My head sank as another wave of guilt washed over me. I

wanted to say something, to apologise for what happened, but I knew that mere words would not be enough. The damage was done. All I could do was make amends through my actions. 'I understand,' I said quietly. 'I will do everything in my power to earn your trust.'

She nodded slowly, her steady eyes still on mine. Then her gaze turned cold again, as icy as the North Sea's waters. 'But just to make absolutely sure you don't betray us, Cwenhild and I will join you on your mission.' She pointed at the taller woman, a blonde, skinny girl our age, a Saxon by the sound of her name. 'If you end up betraying my group . . . .' She made a slicing motion across her throat. 'No place in England will be safe for you.'

Ciara agreed to meet up the next morning on the road south. Thegn Ralf had informed me that the Bishop of Elmham would be attending a significant meeting called the Witan, in London. This Witan was apparently a gathering of all the nobles in the land, who would come together with the king to make crucial decisions for the realm.

We said our goodbyes, me riding back to the inn to finally get some sleep. The following day would require all our energy again, for we would finally start our real purpose, our quest to obtain the holy relic of Saint Willibrord, the first bishop of Wiltenburg. And I somehow had to convince Robert to allow two ladies to accompany us, something I was sure he would never accept.

Chapter Eighteen

After a decent rest, Robert and I stood outside packing the horses at dawn. As Gerold came out with a bag of food, I fumbled with my saddle, trying to find the words to convince my mentor to allow Ciara and Cwenhild to travel with us.

Robert growled at Gerold to hurry up. The old veteran had used a part of his reward to buy a palfrey in town, allowing Gerold to ride her while Robert rode his own destrier. The only problem was that Gerold could hardly ride and took his sweet time mounting the animal.

Still unsure what to say, the sight of two friends I thought had departed took me aback. Trollmann and Frethirik emerged from the stables, each leading a horse by its reins, their smiles stretching from ear to ear. They halted in front of us, fully packed, ready to start a lengthy journey.

'What is this then,' I mumbled. 'Where are you two going?'

Trollmann pointed at Frethirik. 'His fault.'

My best friend beamed, his hands shaking as he spoke. 'Reginhard, I couldn't let you travel alone. I told father how I wanted to be like him and Salaco. I want to help you, my vrindr,' he exclaimed. The sheer surprise of my best friend joining me on this journey left me momentarily speechless. My voice faltered as I struggled to find the right words to respond, my lips frozen in astonishment.

'Fine, you Viking heathens, you can tag along,' Robert grumbled, shaking his head. 'But we need to start moving immediately.'

But even the stern Norman veteran couldn't hide his smile as he tugged his reins. 'We must reach London before those idiots from Echternach discover the whereabouts of the ring. Let's move, men.'

Trollmann and Frethirik mounted their horses in silence. Even Gerold managed the feat once his horse was under control. Yet, as we rode out of town, I knew I had to inform the group about our new companions waiting for us somewhere down this road. What could I say that would make sense? How would they accept two women suddenly joining us?

I shifted uneasily in my saddle, but after taking a deep breath, I cleared my throat to speak up. 'Friends, I must share with you some news. In fact, we are not alone on this journey, as some others wait for us down this road.' As I spoke, my companions exchanged glances, their eyes filling with questions.

'Okay so who are these people?' asked Frethirik, breaking the uneasy silence.

'They are two travelers who I asked to join us on our journey,' I replied. 'Their names are Ciara and Cwenhild, and they are familiar with the road to London.'

Robert scowled, his eyes piercing mine with hellish intensity. I could also see the skepticism on my companions' faces, but I knew it was important to be transparent with them. We were all in this together, and trust was the key to our success, that much my father had taught me.

'Look, of course we must be cautious,' I added, trying to appease Robert. 'We do not know these travelers, and we must keep our guard up. But I reckoned we could use locals to point us to London, even though Thegn Ralf claimed the roads to be of good quality. They know this land and we do not. I used some of the silver I earned to pay them as guides.'

Robert couldn't take it anymore. 'They are bloody women, Reginhard. Since when are you interested in wenches of the road? How can we possibly trust that kind of folk?'

Trollmann nodded vigorously. 'True, Reginhard. Whores kill you in your sleep if it suits them. We have silver, which they'll want. However much to your liking they must have been, we cannot trust such people to guide us to our destination. They could well lead us into a trap.'

Of course, I understood their concern, but they didn't know what I knew. They hadn't seen all these wretched thralls at that camp. We had already faced numerous challenges, and adding two more travelers to the mix would only complicate things further. But I also knew we couldn't turn our backs on those in need, and these two needed our help.

'You have a point, Trollmann,' I said. 'We need to be cautious and not trust them blindly of course. But we also can't turn our backs on those in need, and I promised these women we would accompany them in exchange for their knowledge of the road. We'll have to find a way to ensure our safety while also helping them.'

Frethirik chimed in, 'Perhaps we can take turns watching them at night while the others rest. And we can always keep a hand on our weapons in case of betrayal.'

Trollmann grinned at my friend. 'I think you have something else in mind Frethirik.'

Frethirik started to protest, his head turning into a beetroot. 'No, that's not true.'

'Enough!' Robert demanded. 'Only one person makes decisions here, and that person is me. Look, you little brat,' his malevolence directed at me, 'I do not care what you throw your pennies at, wenches, ale, or anything else your youthful spirit desires. But you do not make any more decisions before asking permission.'

He took a deep sip from his alesack, a long silence ensuing, his scowl a battlefield of anger versus rage. Finally, however, Robert's tense back relaxed, a deep sigh ending his inner war. 'All right, fine, these wenches can come with us, but none of you . . . .' He turned around in his saddle, pointing at me, Frethirik, and Gerold. 'Not one of you lays a hand on them. Our goal is clear – the relic and the riches it will bring us. It is our duty to Wiltenburg and our path to advancement. We must keep our focus on that and nothing else.'

He turned around again, drained the alesack, and kicked his spurs, his horse's hooves kicking up dust behind him. We reached a forest, trees slowly swallowing our party, yet there was no sign of the two women. I swallowed, afraid something might have happened to them. We were supposed to meet on the road to London, yet according to Thegn Ralph, once we passed this forest, we would already reach Colchester, so we should have seen them by now. Had they decided not to come in the end?

As we entered the forest, I couldn't shake off the unease. The dense trees seemed to close in on us, casting dark shadows on our path. The deafening silence was broken only by the sound of our horses' hooves on the forest floor. But then, out of nowhere, the two women emerged from the trees, bows hanging on their shoulders. A wide grin crossed Ciara's face as she addressed our group in a voice ringing with confidence. 'Sure took your sweet time, Reginhard.'

Robert frowned at her, unable to speak for a moment. His scowl returning, he faced me, hissing, 'These women are armed, little brat. Where the hell did you find these?'

'Well Robert, that is why I considered them excellent guides. Who knows what other thralls hide out in this forest? Who knows what the road to London has in store for us? They looked like they knew the area.'

The veteran halted, unsure how to deal with the situation. Normally resolute and a natural leader, he now took his time to assess the women. He ordered Gerold to hand him another alesack, as he slowly got off his horse. Then he stared at them, mainly at Ciara, the most commanding presence. He took in the women's eyes, weapons, clothes, how they carried themselves, and even the mud on their faces. For a moment, I feared he realised where I had found these two wild spirits.

But then he just nodded. 'Let's carry on then.'

Even though we continued on horseback, the women marched in front of us, nimble and quick on their feet. I was sure the bread I had given them had done them some good, and I wondered if I even possessed the stamina to match them on foot. While half-famished, they ran in excellent physical condition.

Fortunately, my fears of ambush proved unfounded as no more thralls emerged – or didn't dare to – in the deep forest between Ipswich and Colchester. After passing through the last trees, we arrived at gently rolling hills filled with the bleating of young sheep. A hamlet here or there, housing thin creatures eying us suspiciously, was all the human activity we encountered until the walls of Colchester emerged in front of us. By now, after a good twenty miles on the road, we stopped in an inn on the edge of town. Robert was so focused on reaching London that he didn't allow us to enter Colchester, commanding us to rest at the inn.

In the afternoon, we marched on, ready to complete thirty miles that day, the maximum one could travel on roads made of dirt and pebbles. Frethirik and I offered our horses to the women while Trollmann recounted stories of the Romans of old, who had built these roads and many towns in Britain. We were exhausted when we trudged into some insignificant village called Witham, where we rested in another sober inn for the night. The women kept their distance, and whenever Frethirik looked at them, Robert gave him a sharp smack.

The next morning, we awoke early for another punishing day of travel. Robert made it abundantly clear that we had to cover forty miles that day, and we all understood that we had no choice but to push on hard to gain on the Echternach agents. We set off at a thunderous pace, our horses galloping along, the women now rotating on our horses' backs. The miles flew by as we urgently rode toward London. As we passed through the trading village of Celmeresfort, we saw the hustle and bustle of merchants and traders conducting business. The town was a hub of activity, with people from all over the region coming together to trade goods and share news.

Yet, we didn't stop. We had a mission to complete, and so we pushed onward. The long, grueling miles tortured our weary bodies, but we didn't falter. We just had to obtain Willibrord's ring before the Echternach agents could.

As the sun began to set, we approached the outskirts of London, the city's massive walls rising up in front of us, a towering testament to the power of the English capital. Relief washed over me as we completed the grueling forty-mile journey in just one day, a nearly impossible feat in Frisia. The well-maintained roads of England had proven to be a boon for our party, and we could finally rest and regroup in this sprawling metropolis. But our mission was only about to start, for it was here in London that we would finally meet the Bishop of Elmsham at the Witan and learn the whereabouts of Willibrord's ring.

The weight of our quest bore down on me as we rode towards the city, where the ring's fate would intertwine with ours. We needed to be at our best to navigate the treacherous waters of intrigue, as the Echternack monks were probably already there. And I was sure they would do anything they could to make things difficult for us.

Chapter Nineteen

As we approached the gates, we heard the hustle and bustle of the city behind the walls. Once we stepped inside, we saw merchants haggling over prices, vagabonds begging for alms, and well-equipped warriors marching through the streets. The noise and commotion overwhelmed me, the sheer size and diversity of the place richer than anything I had ever seen. The buildings were constructed from a mix of materials, some made of wood, others of stone, and many adorned with intricate decorative carvings. Although significantly larger than Wiltenburg, London's winding streets were narrow, with the occasional alleyway leading into complete darkness.

Thegn Ralf instructed us to go to the yet unfinished Westminster Abbey and ask the clerics to point us toward the Bishop of Elmham's residence. When we approached, the abbey's magnificence outshined Wiltenburg's most splendid church. The cathedral's gothic spires and intricate detailing exuded a sense of sacred reverence as a place of worship.

Everyone but Robert gaped at the building, and of course, Trollmann couldn't help but enlighten us with his knowledge. 'They say that King Edward swore that if he ever gained the crown of the kingdom of England he would make a pilgrimage to Rome. Yet as soon as he became king, his duties prevented him from doing so, which prompted him to invest in an abbey instead.'

I nodded. Edward had greatly extended the church we now faced and watched its progress daily from his luxurious palace next to it, now also emerging fully into our view. It made sense then that he chose the large town of London to hold the royal councils, the Witans. Unlike his predecessors, who preferred Winchester, the king stayed at this residence for a significant part of the year.

Gerold's eyes widened as he took in the grandeur of this Westminster Palace. The building stood like a keep, with towering walls made of stone and a steep roof of slate tiles. Delicate decorations on the walls featuring images of mythical creatures, noble warriors, and important historical figures adorned the palace; clearly, no expense had been spared in its construction.

The sunlight glinting off the stone walls of Westminster Abbey cast a warm glow on the surrounding area. Several clerics and courtiers bustled about their daily business, unfazed by the magnificence of either building. We approached the entrance, its reverence overshadowing us, its ornate carvings depicting scenes from the Bible and various saints. The imposing entry welcomed us with large open doors adorned with iron fixtures. The sound of the church bells echoed through the air, adding a certain solemnity to the moment of our arrival.

We dismounted and made our way inside, leaving the horses with Gerold. The serene beauty of a yet unfinished interior greeted us, with its vast nave and rows of columns stretching towards an uncompleted apse. The air thickened with the scent of incense while the soft glow of candles illuminated the shadows of the church.

Several clerics were deeply absorbed in prayer and devotion until a scowling priest stepped forward to bar our way. His eyes narrowed as he demanded to know our purpose. I stepped forward and introduced myself, explaining that we were travelers seeking the whereabouts of Bishop Æthelmær of Elmham. I showed him the letter from Bishop William as evidence.

The priest eyed the seal on the letter, mumbling to himself. 'Very well,' he said after concluding the letter was genuine. Then he waved a hand in the direction of a nearby servant. 'This way.'

The servant led us through a winding street outside the abbey until we arrived at a large, stately manor. This comfortable-looking wooden residence had a thatched roof and a small inner garden filled with colourful flowers and herbs. The structure had a sturdy wooden door and small openings with shutters that allowed for a hint of sunlight to seep through. Though a far cry from the grandeur of Westminster, it still exuded a certain charm that made it inviting.

The priest knocked on the door, and a moment later, it was opened by a round-faced, kindly woman who introduced herself as the bishop's housekeeper. After we told her of our purpose, she smiled. 'Welcome,' she said, ushering us inside. 'The bishop has been expecting you.'

After a moment, the housekeeper reappeared, then led us to a room where Bishop Æthelmær of Elmham opened the door. He had a commanding presence, wearing a massive silver cross over a red cassock, his eyes radiating intelligence as he scanned our faces. He greeted us warmly, pointing inside, where a simple but elegant room greeted us, its central fire casting a comforting glow on the tapestries that adorned the wall.

The bishop invited us to sit down, his voice booming with enthusiasm. 'Greetings travelers, I am Bishop Æthelmær.' After the servant handed us some wooden cups with brown ale, his eyes lit up in the fire. 'Welcome to my humble London residence friends,' he began. 'I am told that you are the agents sent here on behalf of my colleague from Wiltenburg?'

'It is true,' Robert responded. 'My name is Robert of

Wiltenburg, and this is Reginhard of Veenkoop.' Then the Norman immediately turned to our business without even bothering to introduce the rest of our group. 'We're in the service of Bishop William to obtain information about the holy saint Willibrord, the Saxon bishop who civilized our people. My liege learned that some of his belongings had been returned to his native Northumbria. He sent us to find a certain relic connected to the saint, his ring, to be precise.'

Æthelmær smiled as if welcoming relic hunters was an everyday occurrence to him. 'True, true,' the bishop responded. 'In fact, this relic was documented a few years back, and fortunately I know just the man you need to speak to.'

His answer struck me. 'Great, my lord bishop, who might he be, the bishop of York perhaps?' Robert asked, his brows raised.

Æthelmær shook his head. 'It would be logical to assume that the archbishop of York, Cynesige, has information of a saint from his region but he is presently not in Northumbria, but in Rome, to receive his pallium.' He sighed as if it couldn't be helped. 'However, after your liege contacted me I have asked around the dioceses of England and learned something very valuable. I happen to know who owns the ring you seek, and it is not the Archbishop of York.'

Bishop Æthelmær paused to look into his cup, contemplating for a moment. 'Actually gentlemen, let's discuss how we can help each other at this point. You see, your lord bishop offered me some settlers and a good sum of denars if I help him obtain Saint Willibrord's ring. The settlers should have arrived by now, but they will only hand over the silver when the ring is safely in your hands.' He crossed himself. 'Your bishop is quite the negotiator. But the Lord knows my poor diocese is in dire needs of such funds.' The bishop looked at Robert, a smile covering his mouth.

'I know of one person who can help you, Robert,' Bishop Æthelmær continued. 'My colleague, the Bishop of Hereford, is a specialist in English saints. He admitted to me that he owns Willibrord's ring and, like me, could use some funds for the construction of a new church. We agreed to split up the silver your settlers hold for us. So your bishop will be satisfied when you are handed the ring, and Bishop Aethelstan of Hereford and I divide the silver he offered us. All benefit from this deal.'

The bishop spread out his arms. 'Go with my blessing,' he said, handing us a letter. 'You are hereby given full authority to act as you see fit in my name. So make sure you get that relic, Robert and Reginhard, for the benefit of the church in both our lands.'

We thanked Bishop Æthelmær and took our leave, eager to continue our quest for the relic. Stepping outside, my heart filled with energy, the afternoon's cool breeze greeting us as we discussed our next goal. The bishop's words echoed in my mind, and I felt the weight of his trust and expectations on my shoulders. Bishop William's face emerged too, his stern look bearing down on me, reminding me of my responsibilities to the church.

The bustling, narrow streets rang with the sound of carts and horses. Robert clutched Æthelmær's letter of authority tightly as my thoughts lingered on the relic and the challenges ahead. Although I had no idea what Hereford would be like, I knew our journey would be difficult, requiring us to use all our skills and wits to succeed.

We crossed the Thames Bridge, where assorted vessels sailed up and down its waters. The sunset cast a golden glow over the city as we trudged to a tavern nearby. As we enjoyed a cup of cool ale, Robert emerged from a crowd gathered around a bard reciting Beowulf. He quickly sat, his eyes darting to a table across the room.

'Fellows, we have a problem,' he said in a hushed tone, pointing to a shadowy figure sitting with a massive warrior. The pair sat in silence, the mysterious figure occasionally whispering to the soldier. While we could not distinguish the cloaked individual's features, the warrior appeared around thirty summers old, with a brown mustache and short-cropped hair.

'The tavern keeper just informed me that those are the Echternach men, a monk named Gerhard and his guard Fokko.'

Frethirik raised one brow. 'Huh, who are they?'

The Norman rolled his eyes. 'Dammit, they are also after the ring you fool. And the bloody tavern keep just told me they leave for Hereford at dawn, just like us. So they know where it is and god knows they may already be in contact with that Bishop of Hereford. They might have offered the man more silver, meaning they could snatch it away before our very eyes.'

My hands tightened into fists as Robert's words sank in. We finally caught up with the Echternach men, which meant that we now faced stiff competition. The massive warrior certainly looked like he knew his business, and we couldn't afford to underestimate either of them. The race was on, and I knew we had to be more cunning than our rivals to obtain the relic.

The thought of failure filled me with dread, and I envisioned Bishop William's stern gaze. We had come so far and overcome so many obstacles to get to this point; the prospect of coming up short at the last hurdle felt too much to bear. I looked at Robert, who returned my gaze with complete confidence; we had to succeed for the sake of the church and for our own honour. Inhaling deeply, I glanced at my comrades. We knew what was at stake and were ready to do whatever it would take to come out on top. We huddled together, the bard's voice in the background fading into a distant hum, as we prepared to face our rivals in the race to Hereford.

Chapter Twenty

As the first light of dawn broke through the horizon, we set out on our journey. One of Æthelmær's priests waited for us outside, dressed in a simple brown tunic and with a frown to match. He pointed a hand at some mules, pacing briskly ahead of us, his steps confident and purposeful.

'Here,' he grunted, gesturing towards the two smallest mules tethered to a pole. 'You women mount these. This way you won't slow us down.' Then, without another word, the priest turned on his heel, leaving us no choice but to follow suit.

Rain poured down as we moved out of London's gates, fields greeting our approach. After trudging the mud-soaked road through numerous meadows, the scenery around us changed rapidly, the rolling hills of the countryside giving way to patches of woods here and there. We passed through the Chiltern hills, its green slopes stretching as far as the eye could see. Not once did we spot the Echternach agents.

On the second evening of our journey, we arrived in Oxford, the town looming before us as we made it out of some woodland. We proceeded to an inn, where we rested briefly and replenished our supplies before continuing our journey the following day. From there, we set out to reach Gloucester, the rolling hills slowly giving way to wide-open plains and farmland. We passed through numerous small villages, where children interrupted their daily chores to greet us with mouths open. At one hamlet, a boy kept racing us, his flushed face panting until he finally stopped. Frethirik waved at him, throwing an apple into the boy's hands. 'Take me with you,' the boy shouted, jumping up and down. 'I want to be a warrior too.'

By evening the next day, we made it to Gloucester, a bustling town. We settled into yet another inn for the night, resting our weary bodies. We rose early, eager to reach Hereford as quickly as possible. Our guide led us out of the town onto a well-traveled road that took us west, where dense forests dotted hillsides and winding rivers cut through the land.

As the sun hung low in the sky, the castle of Hereford appeared on the horizon, its walls and towers surrounded by hovels. We urged our horses on, eager to finally reach our destination and speak to the bishop of Hereford. Once we drew closer, I glanced at the ramparts, where dozens of armed warriors stood guard. We slowed our pace, not wanting to draw too much attention. My heart raced; we were so close, the ring truly within our grasp now.

Yet, as we neared Hereford, something struck me as odd. Why was there actually a castle here? I thought, not having witnessed any others in England.

It was as if my mentor had read my thoughts. 'The Lord Ralph commands here,' Robert grinned. 'Good thing to be in the presence of some Normans again.'

'Yes, I heard this earl Ralph has quite a number of Norman followers,' Trollmann added, his eyes widening. ' I heard he is one of the Frenchmen that traveled with King Edward when he returned from his exile in Normandy to get crowned in England. The earl got rewarded with land and built a Norman style castle here.'

We passed the numerous hovels on the way to the castle gate. The peasantry had clearly sought out the protection of the walls, hoping to find some relief from the Welsh raids on the county. They peered at us, squinting their eyes, some even spitting on the floor as we neared them, others whispering to their neighbors. Despite the relative safety that the castle walls provided, a strange unease hung around town. The constant threat of attack loomed over these people, and it seemed they lived their lives in a state of constant vigilance.

As we trudged through the castle town, we saw peasants going about their daily business, tending to their crops and livestock, some trading goods. Although not as grand as London, Hereford was still a bustling, vibrant community, and I admired the resilience of those who lived here in such daily danger. Although so different from Frisia, I felt I understood them, their constant alertness a reminder of the storms that plagued my own kin.

Robert grunted, completely ignoring the stares launched in his direction. 'Look Reginhard, this castle has a great view of its surroundings. Ralph proves smart; he cut down all the trees near the place to provide timber for construction, but that also enabled him a better view. This way he can see the Welsh approach from miles away.'

Trollmann nodded. 'And he created easy targets for his crossbowmen.'

We passed a bustling market fair selling goods. There, Normans, Welsh, and English alike were all drawn to the abundance of Herefordshire's produce, from the ever-popular woolen clothes to succulent pears and apples, various meats, and locally brewed ale and cider. My belly rumbled at the scent of roasted meats and freshly baked bread, and laughter and conversation filled my ears. We could all use some companionship, food and ale by now.

We dismounted, and Robert bought bread to still our hunger. People from all walks of life mingled, traded goods, and shared stories. A heartening sight. And despite the constant threat of danger, life in Herefordshire simply went on for the men and women in these borderlands.

After filling our bellies, we retired to a quiet corner of the fairground to discuss our plans. We had to find answers to the ring's whereabouts, no matter the cost. Our guide told us he would speak to the bishop the next morning and suggested we rest for the night first.

Settling into an alehouse, I felt relieved at finally arriving in Herefordshire. It couldn't take too much effort then, I thought, together with Æthelmær's agent and Robert, to convince Bishop Æthelstan to hand over the ring. I knew Bishop William offered serious coin; besides, Bishop Æthelmær had already been in contact with Hereford too. I hoped and prayed Bishop Æthelstan would allow us to buy the relic from him. I closed my eyes, mumbling to myself. 'We'll come home like heroes.' That, I was sure, would have made father proud.

Sipping our ale, we asked the locals for any information they might have on the ring. But they offered only vague rumors, leaving us unsure which could be true. Ultimately, only Bishop Æthelstan had the answers, and we simply had to wait a little longer to meet him.

Yet then, just as we prepared to retire, the door to the alehouse swung open with a loud creak, the chatter of the patrons coming to an abrupt halt. Two shadows blocked the doorway, their silhouettes outlined against the bright light of the torches. One wore a hood over a monk's robe, and the other was clad in a gambeson, wielding a sword. My hand flicked to Robert's shoulder, my other one pointing at the door. 'Robert, it's them. It's the Echternach men.'

I steeled myself as the duo strode towards us – their intense gaze fixed on our group. It was clear that they were here for one reason – the relic. As they drew closer, the warrior's hands resting on his weapon, I instinctively reached for the dagger at my side, ready to defend myself.

The Echternach men stopped a few feet from our table, their eyes flickering over each of us. I could feel their gaze piercing through me, assessing my every move.

'You again,' the warrior growled, his hand tightening around the hilt of his sword. 'What are you Frisians doing here?'

My throat was dry as I spoke, but I kept my voice steady. 'We're just passing through,' I replied. 'We have business in Herefordshire.' They didn't blink once but just kept staring. The hooded man suddenly turned around. 'They're from Wiltneburg. I have seen that Norman before with the bishop.'

Strangely, the Echternach men strolled straight back through the door. We looked at each other, our eyes wide, my mind boiling with thoughts of what would come. As reality kicked in, I knew we were in for a fight. We just had to be careful; if the Echternach men were already here, they would likely try to reach Bishop Æthelstan too. Somehow, we had to find a way to find him before they did.

That night, I couldn't sleep. What could the Echternach's men offer Bishop Æthelstan in exchange for the ring? The warrior was clearly well-versed in the art of war, and they both had a certain air of danger about them that was hard to ignore, but did they carry enough coin? We had come too far to give up now. I wanted to make Father proud and bring Willibrord's ring back to where it belonged.

Chapter Twenty-One

We rushed straight to Hereford's church the next day, hoping to arrive before the Echternach agents. Approaching the bishop's complex, I saw his cathedral rising in the distance. As we neared, the monk and the warrior from Echternach, whom I fully expected to be around, were nowhere to be seen. My heart swelled as we drew closer to the cathedral. Somehow, I felt Willibrord's ring, this divine place a fitting house to a holy relic.

We stood in front of two massive doors flanking the church's entrance, each intricately carved with scenes from the Bible. As we stepped inside, the interior of the cathedral light flooded from the simple but large windows, illuminating the intricate frescoes and tapestries that adorned the walls. The scent of incense and candles welcomed us as chanting and prayer echoed through the halls.

We crept towards a large altar, our footsteps thumping softly in the vast space of the cathedral. In its centre, an elderly man dressed in red bishop's attire stood before the altar, his head bowed in deep prayer. With hands folded, a larger monk accompanied him, his left arm locked with the older man's right. This had to be Bishop Æthelstan of Hereford, I thought.

The bishop stood there frail and feeble, and it was clear that he couldn't stand on his own. As we drew closer, he seemed entirely unaware of our presence, lost in the depths of his devotion. We neared slowly, careful not to disturb his prayers. The reverence of this bishop humbled us, so we just stood there in silence, watching as the bishop and the monk continued their supplications. Then the bishop suddenly mumbled softly in Latin, crossed himself, and tapped the monk's shoulder. About to move away, the monk finally noticed us, whispering something in the bishop's ear. The bishop turned around, his cloudy eyes giving away his blindness.

Thin, pale lips parted to reveal his yellowed teeth as he spoke in a low, gravelly voice. 'Who are you, and what brings you to this holy place?' he asked, his sightless eyes scanning around.

We stood before him, unsure of what to say. His presence imposed a profound divinity, overwhelming even Æthelmær's servant into a meek silence. The monk just peered at us, leaving the bishop to do the talking.

Æthelmær's priest took a deep breath, swallowing hard. 'My lord bishop, I am guiding a group of men in the service of the Bishop of Elmham. They are here on account of a holy relic. It is in the interest of both our churches to strike a deal with these men, who themselves operate on orders from Bishop William of Wiltenburg. My own liege sent you a letter with details about the relic they seek; it concerns Saint Willibrord's ring.'

Bishop Æthelstan's eyes widened. 'Ah, of course, of course,' he said, nodding. 'I did receive that letter and the offer it detailed. Please, gentlemen, follow me to my chambers. That's where some of my collection can be found.'

He led us through the ornate hall of the cathedral, pointing out from memory the various artworks and artifacts that adorned its walls and alcoves. Our footsteps crunched softly on the gravel floors as we approached the bishop's private chambers. Across the hall, we entered a spacious room, my eyes drawn to the countless treasures on shelves, pedestals, and tables. The flickering candles cast a warm, golden glow over the room, illuminating the various jewelry, staffs, and clothes on display. The dancing flames brought their delicate details into full view, each item gleaming and sparkling.

We moved slowly around, the soft rustling of our clothes and the occasional creak of the floorboards the only sounds that disturbed the peaceful atmosphere. It was as if we had stepped back in time, surrounded by the artifacts of a long-lost era.

The bishop's creaky voice broke the serenity. 'These are the many holy relics that have come into my possession over the years.' He kept trudging on, the large monk practically carrying the old man, until they reached a chest that the monk opened. With a gentle smile, Bishop Æthelstan reached into the chest to retrieve a small black box. At first glance, it appeared unremarkable, plain, simple, with no ornamentation or markings to suggest any significance.

But as he turned to face us, he grinned, so I knew this box had to contain something special. With deliberate care, he lifted the lid, revealing a delicate gold ring, its surface adorned with intricate patterns and a flawless amethyst dancing in the torchlight. Upon closer inspection, I saw Latin words carved on its edges, reading Patriarchae Traiectum Willibrordus.

The bishop laughed. 'Can you read it? It proves this was the ring of Bishop Willibrord of Wiltenburg, back then still referred to as Traiectum, its Roman name. This is Saint Willibrord's ring,' he smiled, holding it out in front of him. 'A precious relic I procured from an Irish priest who knew nothing of its significance.' The bishop smirked. 'He couldn't even read Latin, the barbarian, but I realised what it was as soon as I laid eyes on it. It must have ended up there when the Great army of Vikings raided Northumbria over a century ago. These Vikings from York had much contact with Dublin, and it must have ended up there, in the dusty library of a

Gaelic priest.' Bishop Æthelstan chuckled again. 'But they didn't even know what they had in their possession.'

The bishop's cloudy eyes widened. 'It is said to possess great power you know, capable of warding off evil and protecting those who wear it.'

As I awed at the ring, the bishop's voice became hushed. For a moment, we were all caught up in the spell of his words, transported back in time to an era of legends and myths. And when Robert and I held the ring, feeling its weight, I knew we had found a precious piece of Wiltenburg's history, a treasure beyond compare.

After the intriguing show, Bishop Æthelstan shut the box's lid again, returning the relic to its protective case. He then gestured for us to follow him, and we trailed him to his residence, a spacious wooden hall nestled beside the grand cathedral.

When we arrived at the bishop's reception chamber, a man in his early forties with dark hair and a neatly trimmed beard greeted us, a worried frown etched on his thin face. He was dressed in expensive linen, and although he carried a short sword, his slenderness gave the appearance of a weak fighter. As we entered, he straightened up, introducing himself as Earl Ralph, the very ruler of Hereford. His steady voice still exuded authority and confidence despite his somewhat weasel-like appearance.

The bishop's reception chamber itself was a spacious room adorned with tapestries and paintings that spoke of his wealth and power, not unlike his chamber of relics. A large fire crackled in the hearth, casting a warm glow over the room and filling it with the scent of burning wood.

Bishop Æthelstan greeted Earl Ralph and gestured for us all to take place at a large table. As we took our seats, the earl wasted no time telling us what was on his mind. He told us of serious troubles that beset his land, of marauding raiders and lawless bandits who preyed on his people. He spoke of the hardships his subjects endured and his frustration at often being unable to protect them. The earl's words conveyed the weight of responsibility he carried on his shoulders, the same I knew my father had felt for Veenkoop.

After Earl Ralph finished, Bishop Æthelstan addressed us. 'Look, gentlemen from Wiltenburg, I am fully aware of your mission. God knows my poor diocese could use the funds your bishop proposes to forward in exchange for Willibrord's ring, but the truth is both me and the earl have more pressing matters on our minds right now.'

My heart hammered, the fate of our mission depending on his next words. We had come so far and put so much effort into finding the relic. Finally, we sat on the verge of discovering whether or not we could procure Willibrord's ring. As the bishop paused, Frethirik fidgeted with a table knife, his fingers tapping restlessly against the hilt. Trollmann's large eyes flickered to and fro, darting back and forth across the room. Even Robert, usually calm and collected, was fidgeting.

Earl Ralph leaned forward. 'You see, a few days ago, a decision was made at the Witan to outlaw Earl Ælfgar of East-Anglia, on vague charges of treachery,' he explained. 'Infuriated by this decision, Ælfgar gathered a fleet of ships and launched a surprise raid along the entire coastline of Kent, before setting sail for Wales.' Earl Ralph tapped the table with his finger, his face contorting into a scowl. 'And that's when our trouble started.'

He let out a deep sigh. 'The Welsh have started raiding our lands in Hereford,' he revealed. 'At first, it was just a few of their warriors, or teulu, raiding a village or two. But now, the Welsh king's warriors are actively searching for weaknesses. We suspect that Earl Ælfgar has teamed up with the Welsh King Gruffydd ap Llywelyn, and that as we speak they are both preparing for a full-scale invasion of Hereford.'

His voice deepened, his dark brow furrowing. 'Four days ago, I sent a scouting party to Richard's Castle, our most outer defense. But I have heard nothing from them since. I fear that they may have been killed on the road, and that Lord Richard never even received my message. That is why I need some men to travel to Richard's Castle and deliver a new message. I had hoped that you could be of service in this matter.'

Robert glanced at me, a drop of sweat leaving his forehead. 'That is why our problem is becoming your problem,' the bishop added. 'I need you to assist Earl Ralph in conveying his message. And after that, we can negotiate the relic. First help Hereford defend itself, and then you will find me a willing man to your cause.'

Earl Ralph nodded. 'I will reward you with silver as well,' he promised. 'I do not expect the world, but I really need experienced men – trained warriors who can travel through dangerous territory to get my message across. The Welsh are mean ambushers, and the road ahead is perilous. I simply do not have the manpower anymore to send my own personal guard there.'

The earl's eyes implored us. 'We really need you.' Throwing a bag of silver on the table, he promised fifty pennies upon our triumphant return with Richard's message. 'I need to know what is going on there,' he said, raising his voice.

I glanced back at Robert. We had no choice but to accept the task at hand. But it was also our duty to aid those who were threatened, especially in the service of the church, and it was clear that Hereford was in dire need of our help. Robert shook the earl's hand. 'We'll be at your service, Lord Ralph. We'll do all we can to save Hereford.'

Chapter Twenty-Two

As we left the bishop's residence, the whole situation made my head spin, the safety of the women and Gerold, and the danger we now rolled into. Once outside, Robert immediately turned to the women, his voice gruff. 'Look, you two and Gerold will stay here, as your presence could prove a hindrance on the road.'

Ciara's eyes widened as she sneered at his remark. 'You, Norman, do not decide where I place my steps.' Her eyes darted to mine. 'Nor do you, Frisian boy.'

'You provide more danger than help to us,' Robert hollered back. 'Look, we all get that you like Reginhard, but you will only put him in more peril if you join us into a bloody war zone. Now pray for us to return safely.' He pointed a crooked finger, a leftover from one of his battles, in her direction. 'Retire to your lodgings. We will meet up once we're back.'

Ciara stormed past Robert towards Cwenhild, who put a hand on her shoulder. The rest of us whispered a quick prayer. I swallowed. With a heavy heart, I bid my farewell to the women when Ciara suddenly hugged me out of nowhere. I felt my face redden as she kissed my cheek. 'You come back, Frisian, you hear. Don't you die on that road.'

I nodded slowly, my eyes drowning in hers. 'I'll make sure. I promise we'll be careful.'

Then we mounted our horses, ready to ride north towards Richard's castle. Earl Ralph had warned us that the journey would take an entire day, maybe even longer, as the stronghold was located twenty miles to the north.

Despite the light of the morning sun, shadows lurked around every corner of the road, some cast by the trees we passed, others the silhouettes of deer jumping from the cliffs. We rode in complete silence, lost in our thoughts and the sound of our horses' hooves pounding against the dirt path.

As the day wore on, I grew increasingly weary, but we pushed on with Robert thundering out in front. 'The Hereford castle was built, aside from a stronghold against the Welsh, as a block against the Godwinson family, you know,' Trollmann lectured as we rode together in the back of the line. 'The king appointed a foreign earl, the Norman Ralph, and men like Richard le Scrope, who owns the castle we now travel to, to halt the ensuing advances of the mightiest family of the realm.' The Sami shrugged. 'Not that he succeeded. The Godwinsons took power in nearly every county anyway, chief among them Earl Harold.' Trollmann's hand covered his mouth as he whispered, 'They say he'll be king soon.'

Trollmann grinned. 'I doubt King Edward expected any of this five years ago. He likely had no choice in banishing Ælfgar and appointing Earl Harold's brother as Lord of Northumbria. It is all court politics you know.'

'You mean an exiled earl of East Anglia is poised to destroy the western half of the country, all while his family is encircled by these Godwinsons. This land is as volatile as my own, Trollmann.' I stared ahead of us. This wretched country, unlike the flat one I knew, could also be used for ambushes, I thought, my eyes scanning the hills.

The road led steadily into a ravine, high hills surrounding us from both sides. About to remark on the dangers of the terrain, I heard a sharp whistling sound and the unmistakable thud of arrows striking the ground behind us.

'Ambush!' Robert's voice cut through the air, sharp and urgent. We drew our weapons, facing the direction from which the arrows flew. I raised my shield, my heart pounding in my chest. Even though we used so much caution, they still managed to ambush us, dammit.

Our assailers, hidden in the woods of the hills, rained down arrows at us from multiple directions. Our horses reared and bucked, and I heard the terrified whinnying of the animals as they attempted to break free from our control to escape the chaos.

Yet despite this confusion, I kept focused on spotting our enemies, dodging and blocking the arrows as best I could. Still, we had to act fast before either of us or our horses got hit. 'We must escape Robert,' I cried, 'or face the same fate the Germans suffered in Frisia.'

'Yet I fear that they will be ahead of us too, eying the road, Reginhard,' Trollmann cautioned.

'Indeed. They are likely to be positioned on both sides of the roads', Frethirik added. 'They'll be all around us with their horrid longbows while we won't even know where they are.'

'But we must do something,' Robert grumbled over the noise of the whinnying horses.

Then, all of a sudden, we caught a glimpse of movement from the hill we faced. Strangely, about a dozen figures now appeared on the crest of the hill, sprinting down towards us, their weapons drawn. Stupid. Why did they do that?

Robert cried out, 'stand ready lads. They outnumber us, but I know we can take them on. Wait for my signal to charge.' I nodded. We needed these Welsh on flat enough ground to compensate for our fewer numbers.

The Welsh warband approaching us looked ragged, the

warriors dressed in tattered clothes and bearing rusted weapons at best. When I looked again, it got even weirder. They cried out, arms flailing, some even dropping their weaponry to the floor. Their group separated as they barged down the slope, scattering in all directions as if the devil was on their heels. One man stumbled and fell to the ground, tripping over a tangle of weeds. As some of them closed in on us, the warbands' cries grew more frenzied, their eyes wide open.

Hooves thundered from above, and then a group of riders stormed out of the woods behind the Welsh. They rode shaggy but sturdy ponies that clambered down the rocky hill with surprising ease, their riders wielding swords and lances.

While the Welsh warriors still attempted to scatter, the horsemen behind them simply cut them down, one after the other, their horses giving them the advantage of speed. Those who managed to escape this slaughter now came running towards us. I gritted my teeth, glancing at Robert for direction when he screamed, 'Charge.' We lunged forward, our lances pointed at the remaining Welsh, now just a few feet away. As I braced for impact, the horses' hooves hammering the rocky road overwhelmed the sounds of our screams.

The warrior I came at now halted to drop on his knees, his head sunk, his hand folding into prayer. Yet I felt no hesitation, no mercy for these ambushers. I couched my lance, its sharp tip glinting in the sunlight as I took aim. Then I drove it forward, the metal tip piercing the man's chest in a loud crunch. His body went limp, and he collapsed in a heap.

Despite the odds against them, the last three remaining Welsh formed a circle, their backs pressed together. Panting, they faced Robert, Trollmann, and Frethirik, their tattered clothes stained with blood and sweat. One could hardly stand, his leg dripping with blood, while the others held onto their spears, jabbing them at my friends.

Robert targeted the wounded warrior, first blocking his spear with his shield, then driving his sword into the man's chest with a swift strike. The warrior collapsed to the ground, his blood spewing all over the rocky road.

Trollmann lunged forward, his spear thrusting towards the next warrior in the circle. The Welshman parried the blow with his spear, but Trollmann quickly recovered, his second thrust driving through the man's throat.

With only one Welsh warrior remaining, Frethirik charged, his axe raised high. The warrior tried to dodge, but Frethirik was too strong, his weapon crashing through the man's spear and down into his skull with a deafening thud.

I took a moment to catch my breath, surveying the carnage before me, the ground now littered with bodies and blood soaking the grass around us. For a moment, we all just stood in silence, staring at a band of riders approaching us, trying to assess what exactly we faced.

Fifteen men on their ponies, armed in leather and light gambesons, stood a few feet away. They carried spears, swords and small crossbows to be fired from horseback.

Suddenly, Robert turned to us, flashing a grin. 'They're definitely Normans, I can see it in how they carry themselves.' Without saying another word, he slowly trudged to their commander, who stared at us from the front of their line.

As Robert took another step forward, their leader smiled, blurting out, 'Bloody hell, I can't believe it.' He removed his helmet, revealing a man with short-cropped, salt-and-pepper hair framing a strong jawline with a neatly trimmed beard. His sweaty face had dirt all over it, but it couldn't hide the scars etched on his cheeks, his blue eyes taking in my mentor's approach.

Robert let out a cry. 'Richard le Scrope.' He stopped in his tracks, taking in the man in front of him. 'I knew I would meet you again someday. For a moment, I wasn't sure it was you. God, you have turned all grey, man.'

'Good to see you again too, Robert,' Richard replied. His eyes widened as he looked the Norman up and down. 'Heavens, how long has it been?'

'Must have been fifteen whole summers old comrade.'

I watched both veterans embrace, holding each other tightly for a moment. 'What brought you to these parts?' Robert asked, finding his voice again.

Richard shrugged. 'Well, at first I took up service with Earl Ralph. We joined him to his new earldom of Hereford. Then he granted me the right to build a castle as outer defense against the Welsh.' Richard let out a deep sigh. 'But now it's all politics again, Robert. These bloody Godwinsons have made things rather complicated, driving that Earl Ælfgar into a Welsh alliance. I fear matters are rather dire, but let's discuss that later.' He waved at the rest of us. 'Come, you must all be hungry and thirsty. Let's go to my castle, it's near. I will tell you more on the road.'

Richard kicked his spurs, his men throwing some alesacks at us. I caught mine from the air, its pungent smell making my mouth water. Gulping it down while I moved, the liquid immediately soothed my throat, washing away the dryness of the battle.

Robert grunted. 'Back in Wiltenburg I had already heard you built a castle here Richard. It made me wonder what kind of dungheap we would come across. A true lord of the hills heh.'

Robert's laugh thundered through the hills of Hereford, its echoing taking a while to pass.

A while later, our company relaxed in the shade of some trees. 'We have been attacked on all sides,' Richard explained. 'Since a few days ago the Welsh have been probing our defenses, checking weaknesses and ambushing travelers and warriors alike. They also butchered the party from Hereford, the one Robert just told me you were asked to find.'

He waved at the road. 'Anyway, we were on patrol, spotting your party, when you got hit by arrows. That is when we noticed that Welsh scum hide in the bushes.'

'By the way, nice destriers you ride these days,' Robert intervened, glancing at Richard's mounts. 'Bloody hell, Richard. Even our youngsters wouldn't want to touch these.'

Richard shook his head, shrugging. 'Lifesavers here my old battle-friend. These ponies prove adapt at hilly terrain and once you become lord of the hills . . . .' He winked at me. 'You'll see you cannot do without them. They are the way to rid ourselves of the cattle raiders skirting around in the hills. The Welsh have used these horses for time memorial, you know.'

After sharing some more sacks of cider and ale, proper introductions were made between all members of our groups. Then, chatting on, we continued trudging the road north towards Richard's castle. All the while, Richard commanded his scouts to disperse repeatedly, his eyes never ceasing to scan his surroundings. The sun now setting, a silhouette began to loom up before us like a dark, brooding giant on the horizon. As we closed, I realised it had to be the castle, perched on the hill, now casting long shadows that stretched across the surrounding countryside.

The wooden keep towered over a bailey, where I spotted

crossbowmen along the parapets. A village lay adjacent to the castle, where peasants toiled in their fields, their children playing games in front of the hovels. I sighed. Lord Richard had accomplished what every young warrior dreamed about – their own demesne carved out of foreign or known land.

As we passed through the village, most peasants just kept to their chores, their faces stone, though some stopped to curtsey Richard, addressing him in French. When our party approached the castle gates, the drawbridge lowered with a heavy thud, the portcullis slowly rising. Waving at his subordinates, Richard led us through the gates, our party heading straight for the keep.

Looking around the bailey, I felt astonished by this Norman rarity placed on the very edge of England. Most Saxon towns had a stout but simple wooden wall around them, but Richard's high keep stuck out like a sore thumb, like Hereford, a proper castle the way they build them across the channel.

After entering the keep, Richard led us to a large reception chambre, sober but comfortable. A massive oak table dominated the centre of the room, polished to a high shine, where we took our seats. Once we settled in, Richard's servants rushed about, carrying trays of steaming hot food and goblets of wine. The scent of roasted meat, fresh bread, and savory herbs immediately made my mouth water, and we dug in the moment the food reached the table.

Then we explained to Richard what we had experienced so far, Robert handing him the letter from Earl Ralph. After reading it, Richard raised an eyebrow. 'Earl Ralph mentions Earl Ælfgar. I fear that this man is teaming up with the Welsh to attack our border,' he pointed out. 'As I said on the road, they constantly probe our defenses, so I fear they will attack with a greater force soon. And that makes Hereford the most obvious goal, as they will want to loot its wealth.'

Richard's words made my stomach churn. Clearly, the Welsh and the exiled Earl of East Anglia posed a serious threat to these borderlands. The thought of Hereford besieged sent shivers down my spine, an image of Ciara trapped inside its walls emerging before me.

'Then we need to prepare our defenses,' Robert's deep voice growled. 'We just can't let them take Hereford.'

'I know that a few years back, Earl Godwin got banished and then teamed up with the Welsh in return for gold,' Richard said, staring at his goblet. 'The Earl succeeded in convincing King Edward to take him back into service after he had raided the English countryside with his Welsh rogues. And so my guess is that Earl Ælfgar offered the Welsh to loot Hereford in exchange for their assistance in war, just like Godwin did before.' He slammed a fist onto the table. 'So this time, we need to be ready for that possibility. Our mission now is to inform Hereford of any Welsh activity from the north and then march to their aid when an actual army is spotted, one I expect to arrive soon. We just don't know from which direction they'll come.'

His words silenced the room, everyone sinking into deep thought until he continued. 'First, we need to gather intelligence on the Welsh movements. I already have scouts patrolling the surrounding areas. Still, I want each of you to also keep your eyes and ears open for any signs of activity. We must be ready to act at a moment's notice.'

He now looked directly at Robert. 'My old friend, tomorrow at dawn I want you to lead a scouting party north. My expectation is that the Welsh will simply march to the south from Rhuddlan,

King Gruffydd's capital. There he will likely have met up with Ælfgar, who I suspect got there by ship, so their fastest way to strike us is to simply head south into the Shropshire Hills, then march past my castle to get to Hereford. Your job is to report back to me immediately if you come across any Welsh movements.'

Robert nodded thoughtfully, but his cheeks tightened. It would be a dangerous mission, but I knew we couldn't obtain the relic until we crushed this Welsh threat, meaning we now had to assist Richard to the best of our abilities.

Later that night, Richard gave us lodgings in the keep, but my restless mind filled with worries as I lay down. On the one hand, I felt relieved to be safe within the walls of Richard's castle, surrounded by experienced warriors. Yet still, I couldn't shake off the dread lingering in my gut. The thought of facing a fierce and unpredictable enemy like the Welsh made me quiver, my father's stories of ambushed Germans spinning around in the back of my head. As a Frisian, I knew how dangerous hit-and-run tactics could be, which was precisely what we faced. So, our mission included securing the sacred relic and protecting Hereford from a full invasion.

After tossing in bed for hours, I knew that I had to just trust Robert and the others. We were all in this together and had to rely on each other to succeed. As I closed my eyes and drifted off to sleep, I prayed that we would emerge victorious and end the violence plaguing this land. Hopefully, a Hereford in peace would return our sacred relic to Wiltenburg without any more trouble.

Chapter Twenty-Three

As we stepped out of the keep, the pitter-patter of raindrops greeted us, echoing off the thick courtyard walls. Richard, dressed in a heavy cloak to protect him from the elements, stood at the entrance, wearing a broad smile. Behind him, four sturdy ponies stood ready for the journey, their coats slick with rainwater and their saddlebags bulging with supplies.

At the gates, twenty riders waited, all lightly clad in leather and gambeson, their clothes damp from the rain. Despite the dreary weather, their sergeant, a sturdy fellow with a long scar across his nose, barked out orders to his men, who immediately sprang into action, mounting their horses. The sound of hooves clopping against the cobblestones filled the air, and the smell of wet earth mingled with the scent of horse sweat.

With a smirk, Richard handed Robert a sturdy pony, pointing at the group of riders at the gates. 'And now, you too will storm the hills, Robert, like a true Welshman,' he joked.

'Uhm,' Robert seemed unable to speak until he glanced at the pony, patting its neck gently. He inspected it a good while, finally grunting in approval. 'I have to admit, he looks like a bloody sturdy horse. Strong legs, healthy fur, good teeth.' He frowned. 'Bloody hell, I never expected the day I would ride a pony into a war zone.'

Richard shrugged. 'This pony could well save your life today, Robert. And I have one for each of your companions too. Consider it the first payment for services rendered,' he said, his eyes gleaming. 'Just make sure you all stay alive, Robert. I trust my men's lives in your capable hands. You are an experienced commander, my old battle friend, and I know you won't let us down,' he continued.

Richard's voice deepened. 'Our enemies are likely nearby, so as soon as you spot a large enough group, race back to me at once. We stand ready to retreat to Hereford, if necessary. My guess is that they will not even assault the castle, but instead bypass it to raid further inland, continuing towards Hereford as quickly as they can. So we need to stay vigilant and gather as much intelligence as possible to counter their forces.'

With a sharp nod, Robert mounted his pony, patting Richard's shoulder like old friends. 'You always talk too much, Richard. We get it already,' he teased. 'I promise I will do everything in my power to lead this conroi safely.'

Robert rode towards the group with us at his tail. Their sergeant waved at Robert, my mentor shaking his head with a grin. 'Good to see you, Tancred,' Robert said, his face beaming. 'I see you too ride ponies nowadays.'

I think the sergeant attempted to smile, but a scar on his nose made it more of a monstrous scowl. I couldn't help but feel relieved he was on our side.

'Good to see you too, Robert,' this Tancred replied. 'I am happy to ride together with you again, even on these shaggy ponies. I will never forget how you saved me in Normandy.' The sergeant pointed at his horrid scar.

After we shook hands, we promptly rode off into the wet countryside. The simple dirt road we used felt like a treacherous, swampy field, the heavy rain turning the ground into a quagmire, making every step arduous.

In front of me, Tancred and Robert exchanged a brief glance. 'Look, Robert,' Tancred grunted, 'we should probably head to the Shropshire Hills first. It provides a good vantage point of the surrounding area. Even in this rain, we can scan the surroundings from that point.' He sighed, wrenching the water out of his glove. 'It will take us a good while, though – we have to cover at least fifteen miles to get there.'

Robert stroked his chin, his eyes scanning the horizon ahead. 'Yeah, that sounds like a smart choice, Tancred. Better to spot the enemy from up high. But let's avoid main roads, instead sticking to the hills and valleys. This rain provides some cover, but we can't be too careful.'

With that decided, we set off towards the distant hills, our ponies' hooves clattering against the muddy ground. We moved through numerous hills and valleys until, in the late afternoon, we arrived at the outskirts of the Shropshire Hills, a rugged and wild area covered by craggy peaks and steep valleys. As we marched deeper into the hills, we left behind the fertile farmland and rolling hills of the lowlands, the landscape becoming increasingly barren and rocky.

Despite its desolation, these hills still held a wild beauty, with heather and bracken covering the ground and twisted oaks clinging to rocky outcrops. The rain turned the hillsides into a riot of green and brown, with rivulets of water trickling down the rocks to form small streams that flowed into the valleys below. Finally, as the day wore on, we arrived at a barren hilltop overlooking the road leading from Rhuddlan into Hereford. A lone tower stood guard there, ancient as the earth itself, built, perhaps, even before the Romans.

The tower stood tall and circular, made of rough-hewn stone that had weathered the centuries. Its battlements were crumbling, and patches of ivy clung to the walls. Yet from its summit, I guessed we could see for miles in every direction, with the road winding through the valleys far below. Through the rain and biting wind, I gazed at the rugged beauty of the Shropshire hills in front of me, trying to spot any movement.

Robert suddenly gave me a firm clap on the shoulder, breaking the serenity of my moment. 'Why don't you climb that tower, heh lad? You can see better from up high.'

The climb would be easy since we weren't wearing our mail for this mission. And even though the cold rain soaked through my clothes, I didn't want to miss the view from the top of the tower.

With a curt nod, I dismounted to make my way up the winding staircase inside the tower. Worn and slippery steps greeted me inside, making it a struggle to keep my footing as I climbed higher until I emerged at the top, rewarded with a breathtaking view.

The hills stretched out in every direction, rugged and wild, with patches of greenery and rocky outcroppings breaking up the monotony. The road lazily wound through the valleys against a backdrop of scattered buildings and trees.

As I gazed out at the vast expanse of land before me, I felt exhilarated despite the chill of the wind. I had never experienced such an awe-inspiring view, this land so utterly different from my own, its soaring heights completely unfamiliar. I forced myself not to look down but to focus on the valley's beauty.

As my eyes carefully scanned the surrounding area, something caught my attention. I detected a steady movement on the road up north, and as I focused my vision on it, my heart sank to my boots. About twenty riders made their way along the dirt path, their weapons and armour glistening in the rain. That meant only one thing – a scouting party from the Welsh. My head sank straight into my hands. We were almost a day's march from the castle, so either we confront them directly or flee.

I couldn't shout a warning to the men below; I couldn't risk the enemy hearing at this distance. I climbed down quickly, bashing my head against the stone and nearly losing my footing. Hugging the wall, I moved slightly more cautiously, hoping someone would see my descent. Ten feet from the ground, I leapt from the tower and rushed to my mentor, grabbing his cloak tightly. 'Robert, I spotted them; look.' I pointed to the north, the enemy now visible from the foot of the tower.

Robert's expression betrayed nothing. He neither blinked nor frowned, instead just facing the sergeant. 'What do you think, Tancred? Just scouts, a raiding party, or something more?'

Tancred squinted, fumbling his beard. 'Mhhh, not entirely sure Robert. But they look well-armed, so I think these are their teulu, their warriors. That means this could be a serious incursion, perhaps a vanguard even.'

Robert frowned. 'The problem is we have to be sure, otherwise we warn the castle without good reason. We must spot the main army, or risk Hereford getting attacked from another side. We just have to make sure it is the northern path their army takes.'

Trollmann joined us, his gaze fixed on the enemy riders, his eyes widening. 'Let's hide the horses in the scrub, men,' he advised. 'I suggest we wait and observe them for a while longer, just to see where they're headed. The only problem is that it will be dark soon, meaning we should either attack them under the cover of darkness or wait until dawn.'

Robert shook his head. 'Both options are risky, but waiting until dawn could force us between them and a possible approaching army, resulting in a death trap. So I fear our best shot is a night attack.'

Trollmann furrowed his brow. 'Well we could use the cover of darkness to get closer and launch a surprise attack.'

Tancred nodded, glancing at Robert. 'I trust your judgement, Robert. But how do we plan such an attack? Since we do not wear our mail, they are better armed than us this time. We need to be careful.'

Robert reflected for a while, studying the enemy's terrain and position. 'We need to split up and come at them from multiple sides. That way, we can confuse them and attack from different angles. Me and Tancred could take the left flank with half of the men. Reginhard, you and Trollmann can then take the right. Since we don't wear our mail, we can approach them more quietly. That is the advantage we now have.'

The men started mumbling, discussing the plan among themselves. As we huddled together, debating more options, the sun began to dip lower in the sky, casting long shadows across the landscape. Finally, Robert spoke up, his voice low and steady. 'All right men, we don't have much more time, so we need to decide. Who's with me for a night attack?'

I saw hesitation in some of the men's eyes. None raised their hands or spoke until Trollmann stepped forward. 'I'm in,' he said, his voice unwavering. 'I'd rather take the risk now than wait for a potential disaster in the morning.'

Then, one by one, the others nodded their agreement, and I knew I had to follow suit. My father had trained me for this moment, and I couldn't let fear cloud my judgment. 'I'm with you,' I added, trying to keep my voice steady.

Robert nodded. 'Alright then. We'll wait until they make camp, and then we move.'

Chapter Twenty-Four

Robert ordered everyone to wear simple brown or black tunics and gambesons, except for Trollmann, who had swapped his pristine white fox pelt for a menacing black wolf skin draping over his head and shoulders.

To my regret, our crossbows couldn't fire well after all this rain, so the men now grabbed javelins from their saddlebags. A menacing grin spread across Tancred's face. 'Our strategy is simple,' he growled. 'We'll take out as many of them as we can from a distance, before charging them with sword and axe.'

We hid our horses and moved to the enemy camp. The rain subsided, and the day turned dark, allowing us to move undetected. The damp earth under our boots muffled our footsteps, and the muted patter of raindrops from the leaves overhead masked our movements. We pressed forward cautiously, our eyes peeled for any signs of the enemy's presence, our ears alert for the faintest hint of a noise that might betray our position. My heart raced with apprehension as we approached our target, ready to slaughter them to a man.

We stopped in some scrub half a mile from the Welsh camp when I noticed they were clearly no fools. They had camped near the road but in a position that provided some safety. They lit a few fires in a small patch of wood, with tents erected around them. At least five guards were posted around the woods, allowing a good view of the grassy surroundings. Unfortunately, the sky had cleared and stars dotted the heavens making it easier for us to be spotted when we approached.

Robert and Tancred positioned on the left side of the wood, while Trollmann and I took the right, with only a few hundred feet separating our two groups. I closed my eyes as I lay huddled in the woods, waiting until most of the Welsh were sleeping. I felt cold, frightened, and unsure why I found myself in that position again, the relic suddenly feeling very distant. I thought back on my father's words all these months ago, how a first campaign would make overseeing an estate seem like a luxury. 'Pull yourself together, Reginhard,' I mumbled to myself. I had to toughen up. Doubts and worries would only obstruct what lay ahead; we had to strike this warband and find out where their main army marched.

After some time passed, Trollmann held up his hand. 'Everyone wait here a moment, let me take out the first one. Then crawl towards me.'

Trollmann crept forward with his wolf head, his movements resembling the animal he wore over his shoulders. He moved slowly but steadily until he neared one of the guards, stopping just a few feet from the Welshman. I heard a sharp whistle, and then I realised it was Trollmann making that sound. It spooked the guard, who now neared the tall grass Trollmann lay in. He died before he even hit the ground, a javelin stuck in his throat. One down, four to go.

Fortunately, the other guards stood at a considerable distance, facing away from our position, which enabled the rest of us to approach Trollmann's post undetected. The Sami warrior dragged the lifeless body into the tall grass when we neared.

When I reached the Sami, he flashed a toothy grin, his eyes glistening. 'Wanna try now, Reginhard?' he whispered, handing me his knife. 'Robert will take the left side,' he pointed at the woods.

'You crawl along the right edge until you spot the first guard. Kill him and move on. Keep the woods to your left until you see the last man. By then Tancred will charge his men into the camp from the left and I will from this position. When I whistle, we will charge, so make sure you finish that last guard by then.'

I nodded. All fear glided away at that moment, my blood in a battle state. With a grin, I accepted the weapon and began to inch through the thick grass, my senses on high alert. I knew there were still four more guards stationed around the perimeter, and I had to take out at least two of them to help our men gain the element of surprise.

As I inched closer to my first target, I felt the damp earth and grass beneath me. After nearly a hundred feet, I finally caught sight of a Welshman facing the grass. I crept into the bushes so I could get behind him. With a swift and silent motion, I lunged forward, burying the blade into his back. I could hear the knife piercing his tunic and then his flesh. The blade slid smoothly into his body as if cutting through butter, a warm sensation spreading across my hand. I stood frozen in place for a moment, watching as the man slumped forward, his hands grasping at the air as he fell. I pulled the knife out, watching a thick stream of blood flow from the wound, almost silvery in the moonlight.

The man's eyes widened, and I could hear him gasping for breath until a blanket of silence covered his mouth, which gave up its movements. I dragged his body into the bushes before resuming towards the next guard.

After passing about a hundred feet, I noticed a shady movement in front of me. 'Who's there?' a deep voice bellowed. A hulking figure suddenly loomed over me as I lay still in the shadows. In the silver starlight, I could make out some details of his face – a brown mustache and a battle-scarred visage framed by an open conical helmet. 'There you are, you little bastard,' he growled, revealing his towering stature.

In a moment of panic, I flung down my dagger and drew my sword from its scabbard. I now realised that I had no choice but to face him head-on. Despite his formidable size, I tried to calm my nerves and trust my training.

The warrior approached with a sluggish gait, a massive sword in his right hand, until he lunged forward with a surprising speed. I raised my sword just in time to parry his attack, deflecting his blade away from me. The clash of iron rang out in the night, sending shivers down my spine. I braced myself, trying to anticipate his next strike.

The warrior began to laugh, his booming voice cutting through the wind. 'You're just a lad, aren't you?' he taunted me. 'You're no match for me. So I hope you've prepared yourself to die.'

With a fierce glint in his eye, he gripped his sword with both hands and charged, his massive frame lumbering forward. I braced myself as he swung his weapon in a wide arc, the blade whistling through the air with terrifying velocity. Quick on my feet without my mail, I managed to sidestep his attack, bringing my sword down in a swift counterstrike. Our blades collided once again, sending sparks flying in all directions.

Our fight raged on like this, the clanging of our blades ringing out as we fought tooth and nail for the upper hand. Sweat poured down my face as I tried to keep up with his relentless assaults, dodging and parrying his blows with all the skill and finesse I could muster.

Yet, as the battle wore on, I realised that brute strength alone was not enough to defeat this towering warrior. He was not particularly clever, constantly relying on his immense size and raw power to overwhelm me. With every passing moment, I could see more sweat bead on his forehead, his breathing becoming more laboured with every strike.

I decided to take advantage of his fatigue. I dodged as he swung his sword, delivering a swift counterstrike. I struck his armour forcefully, but the iron rings protected him, and he managed to stay on his feet, swiftly attacking once more.

Roaring, he raised his sword high in the air. 'Too slow,' I blurted out, striking a precise blow to his mail-covered knee. His leg buckled under him as he fell to the ground, his sword clattering out of reach. Panting heavily, I stood over him, my sword at his throat.

But then it suddenly struck me – I had seen this man before. His ugly mug and distinctive helmet clearly betrayed his identity. It was the very same warrior who accompanied the monk from Echternach, the one we spotted in Hereford before.

He was here for Willibrord's ring. That's why we hadn't seen them in Hereford when we visited the bishop. They planned to take the relic by force, using the Welsh as a tool to get into Hereford.

Suddenly, my head exploded with pain, sending me reeling backwards. I stumbled to the ground, my sword flying out of my hand. Dazed, I saw another figure standing over me – a shadowy figure blurred in the darkness.

With a sudden burst of strength, the fallen warrior lunged forward, grabbing his sword to make a run for it. The shadowy figure followed close behind, both disappearing into the night.

Lying on the ground, my head throbbed, my body battered. I rose unsteadily, stumbling towards the woods. As I emerged from the trees, I saw the Normans standing triumphant over our enemies. The remaining Welsh fighters sat bound in ropes, their weapons strewn about the ground.

Sighing with relief, I approached our victorious warriors. I could see our men leaning on their weapons, panting but with gleaming eyes. God be praised, I thought, as I crossed myself – we had succeeded in our night attack.

I took in the battlefield, the fallen Welsh fighters, many pierced by our javelins. The air reeked of smoke and blood, and dying cries mixed with the occasional clang as our warriors threw weapons on a pile.

A group of wounded Welsh fighters had been gathered together, their hands bound with rough ropes. Robert stood before them, his sword pointed at a man with long grey hair and a neatly trimmed beard. The man gave Robert a stern look.

Tancred oversaw the binding of the last prisoner. 'Well done,' I said, offering him a nod of respect. 'Your men fought bravely tonight.'

As Trollmann and Frethirik ran over to us, Tancred looked up at me, a smile playing at the corners of his mouth. 'As did you, Reginhard,' he replied. 'But what's that blood on your face?'

'The last guard spotted me,' I said. 'It was that Echternach warrior we saw before in Hereford. Clearly, these Echternach men teamed up with the Welsh. I think they just want to take the relic by force.' Then, I recounted how I overpowered the warrior but got hit on the head. 'I'm fine, just a bit shaken.'

Trollmann examined my wound, nodding. 'You'll live,' he grinned. Frethirik patted me on the back. 'Well done, Reginhard. You fought well tonight. For a moment I thought something had happened. I was about to look for you.'

I approached Robert, still pointing his sword at the greybeard.

'I guess we're about to find out,' my mentor grunted, pricking the blade into the man's neck. Some blood poured out of the skin, and the Welshman winced in pain.

'So who are they?' I asked, peering over Robert's shoulder at the captured Welshmen.

Robert turned to me, his expression grim. 'These are some of the Welsh teulu who have been causing trouble in the area,' he explained. 'They already admitted they raided some nearby villages up north, stealing livestock and supplies. We believe their next words will reveal the location of the main army.' Robert grabbed the prisoner's grey hair, pulling his head back. 'Better speak pal, if you desire to live. Better a prisoner of war than die a torturous death.'

Tugging his tunic, I took Robert apart. 'What will become of them?' I asked.

'Actually, that is up to Tancred and his men,' Robert replied. 'They can decide what to do with them, but I doubt they'll show them much mercy.'

I looked back at the prisoners with a mix of pity and revulsion. Though they had been our enemies, it was hard not to feel some sorrow for their plight. War again proved a brutal affair, and in the end, who really was the winner? I just wanted the relic, none of this needless bloodshed caused by none other than English nobles themselves. And now simple villagers even had to pay in these Welsh raids, just like Veenkoop had.

'AHHH!' the greybeard screamed, clutching his face, as Robert stabbed the man in the eye. 'Where's the main army?' Robert bellowed at the prisoner, his cheeks tightened. 'How far away are they?'

The greybeard let out a whimper, blood trickling down his face. 'They are . . . they are only a few miles away, to the north, following our lead,' he stammered, his voice barely audible. 'Please have mercy on me.'

Robert sneered, his eyes burning. 'Mercy? You Welsh bastards showed no mercy to the people you slaughtered in the villages. Now tell me, what's the size of your army?' The prisoner hesitated, then muttered, 'I don't know exactly, but it must be more than a thousand strong.'

Robert frowned, his voice now raised. 'Tancred, we must act swiftly and warn Richard before it's too late. We must leave everything behind and ride at once,' he declared promptly. He swirled around to face the sergeant. 'And kill them all.'

The Norman Sergeant nodded, his own face mirroring Robert's. His men moved swiftly, their swords glinting in the starlight as they carried out their brutal work. The prisoners, who just moments ago pleaded for mercy, fell on the ground, their blood staining the grass. Iron hacking through mail echoed through the night as our warriors hacked and slashed at the helpless captives. The sickening thuds of swords biting into flesh soon replaced the Welsh screams, their death cries cut short by the merciless onslaught. The unprecedented carnage was one not easily forgotten. I tried to block out reemerging images of Veenkoop in flames, forcing myself to carry on.

After that bloodbath, we all rushed back to our horses, aware that the enemy approached us only a few miles from the north. We had to warn Lord Richard of the impending attack. No one expected the Welsh to march in such a massive force, so the fate of Hereford, and Willibrord's ring, now hung in the balance.

Chapter Twenty-Five

We galloped towards the castle, our hearts heaving with the knowledge of the Welsh numbers. The rain started again, heavy droplets falling from the sky to soak our clothes, but we kept pushing on through the dark night. The sound of thunder and lightning followed us as we rode, reminding me how urgent it was that we warn Richard.

We didn't arrive at his castle until noon the next day, but he already stood waiting for us in front of the gate with twenty riders. Robert bellowed at Richard, telling him everything we learned. Upon hearing the enemy's numbers, Richard winced. His head hung low for a moment before he spoke up.

'Well your news even surpasses my most dire predictions, but fortunately I did prepare for this scenario. I have already sent my son and wife to lead our peasantry to Gloucester, together with all of our food and valuables. The men you see around you are the only souls left from my castle, and we stand ready to move to Hereford at once.'

Richard looked around him, staring into the eyes of each warrior. 'Men, it is time. We knew this moment would come and it seems the Welsh are now coming in full force. Our duty is to return to Hereford at once and defend the town against them. We abandon the castle.'

A stable boy approached with our original horses, which we mounted, tying the new ponies behind us; they deserved a small respite, even though they would still have to ride for twenty more miles. We took until the night to reach the outskirts of Hereford, but we stubbornly rode on, knowing that every mile we gained on the enemy could save Hereford. We had to warn the town quickly so Earl Ralph could muster a proper defense.

Deep into the night, we finally arrived at Hereford, the sentries blowing their shrill horns for all to hear. Panicky voices demanded to know what was happening. Some called, 'Is it the Welsh? Are they coming?' while others nervously eyed us in silence, trying to identify us. Richard called out to the guards, who immediately allowed us access. We thundered to the keep, where Earl Ralph waved us into his castle.

'Well Richard,' the earl grumbled, his reddened eyes betraying his lack of sleep, 'I take it this is no social visit?'

'No, Earl Ralph, I bring dire news.' Richard grunted in response. 'As you must have understood from my son by now, the men you sent a few days ago died on the road, the entire area around my castle already overrun by Welsh patrols. Yet I feared they were only the beginning, so I sent Robert here to lead a scouting party out north. Once there, they beat off a party of teulu and pried vital information out of them.

Richard's voice grew louder. 'My lord, the Welsh marched only a few miles north of the Shropshire Hills, so by now, they could be at my castle already. That means that by tomorrow they will arrive at Hereford.' His eyes widened. 'And my lord, according to the captured teulu, they march with a thousand warriors.' Richard's tone nearly pleaded at this point, his eyes locked on the earl's. 'That means we need the entire county's fyrd, my lord, all available warriors from the shire and reinforcement from Gloucester too. I pray you send messengers to assemble an army here without delay.'

Earl Ralph stood frozen, sweat dripping down his face.

Clearly, he hadn't expected an attack this soon, let alone having to act on such short notice. 'A *thousand* strong, you say?' He fell into his chair in disbelief. 'How, how is that even possible? Since when are Welsh armies this large?'

'Well, King Gruffydd is the first king to unite all of Wales, Lord Ralph. We also know that Earl Ælfgar sailed more than a dozen ships, and he might have followed Earl Godwin's example of enlisting Irish mercenaries too.'

Richard placed his hand on the earl's shoulder. 'But be that as it may you know we still stand a good chance, certainly with our Norman cavalry in place. We just need everyone here on time. So please send messengers right away.'

Still pale, Earl Ralph regained his senses, waving some servants away to fetch his bodyguards. He ordered various men to ride off into the night and raise the alarm throughout the county. 'War has come to our doorstep, men, and we must now defend Hereford with our lives.' His high-pitched voice announced to all standing around us.

Then, the earl's tone suddenly softened. 'Well, you rode all day and night, so you all deserve a rest. I will ready the barracks for your men, Richard, and provide a room for you at the keep. We all bowed at that welcome gesture, much in need of rest, so Robert, Frethirik, Trollmann, and I slowly trudged outside, ready to head to the barracks.

Yet once we stood in the bailey, I suddenly noticed Ciara and Cwenhild waving and shouting at us. Guards blocked their entry to the castle, so I ran up to them, Frethirik hot on my tail.

As Ciara set her eyes on me, they immediately filled with tears. Before I knew what was happening, she threw herself in my embrace. Bemused by this reaction, I didn't know what to do, so I gently stroked her back.

'I feared the worst,' she mumbled as she released herself from our embrace. 'I am so glad you're alive. I thought you had all died. We didn't know what to do when that would happen.'

She looked down, her sadness striking deep into my heart, somehow making her all the more attractive. Then, as I looked past her, I suddenly noticed Cwenhild hanging around Frethirik, reaching up to kiss him. And as my gaze darted back to Ciara, I locked onto the green of her eyes, willfully letting myself drown in them. Without realising it, my lips found hers too, the warm wetness of her embrace washing over my entire body.

By now, Robert, Trollmann, and Gerold were nowhere to be found, and so Frethirik and I joined the girls, slipping quietly into the convent. As we made our way towards their rooms, we had to be extra cautious to avoid drawing the attention of the nuns who ran the place.

Thankfully, our nocturnal visit went off without a hitch, and by morning, we slipped out of the rooms undetected. Frethirik and I breathed a sigh of relief when we returned to our quarters, grateful we had avoided the nuns' gaze. Then we collapsed into a shattering laugh.

The rest of the day proved a waiting game as men from all over Herefordshire tripled into the castle. Most were simple peasants from the villages, who would be organized into what the English called a fyrd, or assembly of militia.

Towards evening, the largest group of men arrived, 300 fyrd-men from Gloucester, led by their burgh-thegn. They marched into the castle courtyard in a simple formation, their shields raised in unison. Their boots thundered on the stone ground as the peasants from Herefordshire watched them filing past. I admitted it was the best-trained militia I had ever witnessed.

The burgh-thegn struck me as an imposing, tall, muscular figure with a stern expression. He wore a suit of chainmail and carried a battle axe on his belt. As he approached the castle gates, he raised his hand in greeting. 'Good evening, men of Hereford,' his deep voice rumbled. 'The Gloucester fyrd has come to offer our support in the coming battle.'

The men nodded enthusiastically, their faces brightening at the vast army. Impressed by the burgh-thegn's strength and solidarity, I grinned as I realised he probably used this show to boost the men's morale.

As the sun began to set, our men settled in for the night, and I knew that the coming day would likely bring with it the start of a battle to determine the fate of Hereford and its people.

Yet, the morning after, the Welsh still hadn't been spotted, so we prepared for their arrival as best we could. The castle was filled with clanging iron, and the shuffle of feet echoed throughout the town as the men gathered and organised into groups. Earl Ralph assigned some to guard duty while he sent newly arrived men to the armoury to collect weapons.

As the day wore on, the atmosphere grew tenser. Everyone knew that a battle loomed on the horizon, the Welsh sure to arrive soon, the uncertainty of what was to come weighing on my mind. By noon, all abled men from Herefordshire had arrived. Richard counted a staggering two hundred horsemen on our side, assisted by five hundred fyrdmen.

The Norman lord voiced all his worries to us as we shared an ale in the barracks. 'Gentlemen, this will not be an easy battle I fear. Our main advantage is our heavy cavalry, but only half of these are trained Normans, the rest were English thegns, and these latter have no experience in cavalry charges. If that prisoner in the Shropshire Hills spoke the truth, the Welsh will outnumber us significantly. Our best bet is actually to just stay behind the protection of Hereford's castle walls and wait it out. We already heard Earl Harold Godwinson is on his way here with his own forces. Once he arrives even a thousand Welsh are no match for our combined numbers.'

He sighed deeply, sipping some ale from his cup. 'Now let's just hope Earl Ralph sees this wisdom too. I can tell you one thing though, he didn't get his lands out of military service, and I am not sure I trust his tactical judgement all that much.' Richard suddenly stood, but before he could leave, Frethirik asked, 'wait. How did he get it then?'

Richard turned around, his brows raised. 'He's the king's nephew of course.' As Richard prepared to move, a blast of a horn shattered the stillness of the castle, jolting everyone into action. Men's voices erupted in a flurry of urgent commands, heavy footsteps thumping as our warriors scrambled to the walls.

Suddenly, a guard's voice boomed throughout the courtyard. 'Our scouts approach, with Welsh riders on their tail.'

A party of English horsemen raced towards the gates, with twenty Welsh riders hot on their heels. As our men closed on the town, the Welsh swirled around. That could only mean one thing, I thought. The Welsh main army was close.

Eyes trained on the horizon, we waited for the main Welsh army to arrive. It began as a low vibration that reverberated through the ground until a clattering horde stood atop the hillside covered with gleaming iron and their banners snapping in the wind as they marched towards the walls of Hereford.

I gasped. The Welsh army was an impressive sight, their

warriors well-armed. They moved in tight formation, their steps heavy and deliberate, ready to lay siege to the castle. We all watched in complete silence, my heart almost pounding out of my chest. As the Welsh army halted, I braced myself for what was to come, praying for God's to help.

I turned back to the barracks, only to spot Earl Ralph stride out of the keep in confident steps, staring around with a wide smile. Standing by his side stood the burgh-thegn and Lord Richard, their shoulders slumped, and their eyes cast downward towards the cobbled stones beneath them.

The warriors in the castle all stared at their leader, their frowns filling the courtyard with questions. As the earl strutted around, his calm gaze taking in the Welsh numbers as if they were a regular occurrence, the men started mumbling and whispering, nervously pointing at the Welsh.

For a few tense moments, Ralph, Richard, and the burgh-thegn stood in silence on the battlements until Earl Ralph spread his arms wide, his voice clear and strong. 'Brothers, comrades in arms, know that God has just spoken to me.'

The courtyard fell utterly silent again as Earl Ralph spoke. The only other sounds were the whinnying of horses and the rustling of the wind as it passed the keep. I clenched my sword, my blood pulsing through my arm.

'I prayed all day for His advice,' Earl Ralph continued, his voice unwavering. 'And just a moment ago, He spoke to me, commanding me what to do next.'

I held my breath, waiting for the earl's next words with bated anticipation. What had God told him? What was the plan?

'Today we will not wait for the Welsh to attack,' Earl Ralph declared. 'But instead we will sally forth and meet them head-on, in the open field. Our numbers may be smaller, but I know our resolve is much greater. And with God on our side, we simply cannot fail.'

As Earl Ralph's words rang out, a wave of encouragement rippled through the men, erupting into a deafening cheer. Their spirits lifted, their faces brightened. Around me, I heard their swords unsheathing while spears pounded on shields in a fearsome rhythm of death.

Waiting until the claps and voices died down again, the earl raised his hand. 'Now we must take the initiative and attack. Let us rout these invaders and give them a thrashing like never before. Today, my brave warriors, we march to glory, and tonight, we feast in victory, rich in spoils. Men of England, let us destroy these Welsh barbarians!'

Shocked, I looked around at my fellow warriors, surprised to see how quickly they had filled with a desire to fight. With a cry, 'For England!' they all followed Earl Ralph out of the castle gates and onto the field of battle.

I swallowed hard, my gaze fixed on Robert's. Like me, my mentor panted, and I could see the rage building in his eyes. With a deep sigh, he shook his head in disbelief.

'Suicide Reginhard,' he grunted. 'Bloody suicide.'

I knew Robert was right. The idea of charging headlong into the enemy was not only foolhardy, but it meant we could well throw away our lives for no good reason. My hands trembled as I struggled to control my emotions, subduing a strong desire to cry out my objection. Despite our misgivings, we knew we simply had to follow orders, or else we could forget about Willibrord's ring.

Richard now passed us, his hand landing on Robert's shoulder. 'Look, old friend,' he said. 'We're duty-bound to obey the earl, but let's not forget ourselves either. I know their teulu are no match for Norman cavalry, but I fear their numbers are simply too great. Be as prepared to retreat as you are to charge. Let's make sure we at least leave this field alive today.'

Robert nodded, waving his hand at the rest of us, indicating to mount up. As we rode out of the castle gates, Ciara and Cwenhild faced us, tears again streaming down their faces. I waved at them, shouting that it would be okay before riding after Robert. I had no other choice than to fight.

Although the earl had widely encouraged the commoners, deep anxiety still hung in the air, and my hand trembled as I clutched my shield tighter. Swallowing away my doubts, I steeled myself for what was to come, knowing my duty was to my comrades and to Wiltenburg. I just had to see this battle through.

Chapter Twenty-Six

Earl Ralph directed our two hundred horsemen to the frontline, positioning the fyrd behind us in support. Robert, mounted on his huge destrier, stood in front of me, while together with Trollmann and Frethirik, I took up position in the second line. I deeply regretted not having a warhorse to charge more effectively, but that would have to wait until I earned one. Nonetheless, as horsemen, our job was clear – to break through the Welsh centre and pave the way for our infantry to finish off the rest of them.

But as I gazed at the enemy troops, a shiver ran down my spine. Their men had formed a tight formation on a steep slope. Though it was difficult to discern details from this distance, they appeared to be primarily light infantry based on their brown tunics. Yet, the glint of iron reflecting from their weapons proved they were still well-armed and very dangerous against our uphill charge.

I crossed myself, letting out a deep gasp. Breaking through such an enormous mass of men was no mean feat. And to make matters worse, they had stationed around fifty horsemen on each flank, ready to encircle us. Realising the odds were clearly not in our favour, my gut tightened.

When Richard put forward the same concerns to Ralph, the earl just shrugged. 'My dear Richard,' the earl's voice grumbled, 'that is why our horsemen ride in two lines, the second line positioned to counter any flanking attacks from the Welsh cavalry.' He waved Richard back into position, his brow furrowing. 'I accept no doubts in my ranks,' he declared. 'You will all obey my commands.'

Earl Ralph took up a position at the front of the army, his eyes fixed on the enemy. 'Usually, their teulu forces are much smaller,' he remarked with beaming eyes. 'The Welsh king is lucky to assemble so many sheep ready for the slaughter,' he boasted, a smirk spreading across his face. His words echoed through the ranks, evoking some chuckles and grins. Still, I noticed our hardy veterans simply arched their eyebrows, shaking their heads.

Richard winced. 'Lord, we don't know what's out there. I implore you to hold off until my scouts can at least confirm no ambush lies in wait,' he pleaded, his voice shaking.

Earl Ralph swirled around, his eyes shooting flames. 'Enough of your cowardice, Richard,' his booming voice roared. 'Imagine the glory of facing them head-on and emerging triumphant!'

He pointed at the enemy horsemen. 'Don't you see the potential glory that awaits us? We could be hailed as heroes, rewarded by King Edward himself. And who knows, after our victory you could well be bestowed with some estates too, Richard.'

Richard frowned but kept quiet. I gritted my teeth. Earl Ralph's stubbornness and focus on glory blinded him to the danger ahead. He callously dismissed Richard's warning despite the man's expertise. His bloody foolishness now put all our lives at risk.

Earl Ralph raised his hand, looked around the ranks one final time, then lowered his arm. Hooves pounding the ground echoed through the valley, drowning out all other noise as we marched in two straight lines, followed closely by the tightly packed fyrd.

The wind raced past me as I clutched my shield and lance firmly. Subduing a tendency to close my eyes, I suddenly heard my father speak. 'You always ride into battle as one son, your knees right next to your comrades.'

Our cavalry thundered into battle with practiced precision,

each line maintaining a near-perfect formation. Though scared to death, blood rushed through my veins. After a lifetime of training, I was riding into battle with my comrades, and the moment felt incredible.

As we galloped on towards the enemy, that feeling only intensified, boosting my confidence in our success. As we drew closer to the Welsh, I could make out the glint of their armour and the flash of their weapons in the sunlight. The upward slope approached fast – we were about to hit them. Winney's breath came hard and fast but without any hint of protest. Her instincts now kicked in, driving her closer to the rest of the herd as we approached the enemy lines.

Nearing the slope, our war cries merged into a deafening roar. I rode right behind Robert, my eyes fixed on the gap between him and the warrior on his right, as I readied myself for the coming impact.

As we couched our lances, countless whooping sounds pierced the air. Suddenly, our front rank abruptly halted, causing confusion and chaos among us. I watched in horror as Robert's body jerked as if struck by a decisive blow to his right shoulder, causing him nearly to drop from his horse. Others around me stopped in their tracks, their bodies convulsing, their blood spouting from various wounds.

Panic quickly replaced the thrill of the charge, Winney now buckling in fear. I tried to steady her, met by horror and disbelief from the warriors around me. A cold sweat broke out on my forehead, the truth hitting me like a hammer; we had been utterly caught off guard.

The sky then darkened, like an ominous shadow looming over the battlefield. I raised my shield just in time to block three incoming missiles. My heart raced as I stared at the arrows protruding from my shield. Thank God I survived that, I thought. Next to me, pale but unharmed, Frethirik and Trollmann shot me worried glances, wildly pointing back to town. A pang of despair stung me as my eyes scanned the battlefield for a way out of this mess.

My attention turned to Robert, who had swirled around, wincing in pain, an arrow lodged firmly in his shoulder. He met my gaze, bellowing at us, 'Back, you idiots. Back to Hereford!' I nodded at him, kicking my spurs hard to retreat behind my mentor, with Frethirik and Trollmann following us closely.

A horn now sounded, with all the survivors fleeing towards safety, Earl Ralph and Richard in front. As we rode back towards Hereford, I glanced behind me, taking in the gruesome sight of the battlefield strewn with fallen warriors. Guilt washed over me at our retreat, but only one man was truly to blame. We obeyed Earl Ralph's rash decision to engage the enemy, and now we all paid the price. How many of our fellow warriors lost their lives because of his foolishness?

Then Earl Ralph, although still in command, fled into the woods with the remaining horsemen, heading straight towards the east. I pointed at them, glancing back at my mentor. 'Robert, look, the earl abandoned the fyrd and his own castle.'

Robert just shook his head. 'Bastard. Well, we just have to rescue the women and Bishop Æthelstan then, Reginhard. We have no choice but to return to Hereford. Let's get that relic.'

As we darted back south, hooves thundered behind us. I peered behind me and saw how a band of Welsh riders now followed us. We urged our horses to go faster, but by the intensifying sound of our pursuers, it was clear their fresh horses were gaining. The thought of capture stung me with dread, especially considering the earlier atrocities we had committed against the Welsh scouts. I fully understood that if captured, we would not be treated kindly.

Yet looking straight ahead, I realised these teulu weren't targeting us. Instead, they charged towards the fyrd, who still held their ground in the field. The Gloucester burgh-thegn bellowed commands, forming his men into a simple shieldwall. But it was clear they could never withstand the Welsh teulu's full force without our cavalry's support.

I forced myself to shake off that worry. We had to focus on Ciara and Cwenhild, and get to the relic as soon as possible. So, with the last of our strength, we raced towards the town, leaving the fyrd to face the Welsh army on their own.

When we reached Hereford, nothing but widespread chaos greeted us. Women and children rushed about, loading animals with their few belongings, their wide eyes looking up at us as they pleaded for help.

We ignored them, heading straight for the bishop's residence, where I spotted Bishop Æthelstan on horseback, standing amidst a throng of priests, monks, and nuns. Gerold, Ciara, and Cwenhild paced among them, their faces pale as ash. When they saw us approach, their eyes filled their tears, and I dismounted, flying into Ciara's embrace. 'You'll be okay, Ciara. We'll get everyone out of here.'

Her eyes were wide open, and she held my face in her hands. 'What's happening out there? They say the earl fled.' I nodded at Ciara. 'It will be okay, trust me.' Then, I looked up at the assembly around us before addressing the bishop. 'My lord, we must leave at once. The Welsh are indeed on their way.'

My message pierced through the commotion, the bishop's

cloudy eyes locking onto mine. He motioned for me to approach. 'What's happening right now, Frisian?' he asked, his voice shaky.

As I explained the gravity of the situation to Bishop Æthelstan, his normally calm demeanor was replaced by a deep frown. The clerical assembly now fell into silence, their eyes fixed on me. Some crossed themselves, others fell to their knees, burying their faces in their hands. Without uttering another word, Bishop Æthelstan signaled for his entourage to follow him, setting us off to the south.

Chapter Twenty-Seven

When we reached the southern edge of town, the bishop spoke to me softly, his voice barely above a whisper. 'Thank God you are here, Frisians. But what about the other townspeople? We cannot simply abandon them to the mercy of the Welsh.'

Just then, Robert let out a sharp cry. Tearing off the arrow stuck in his shoulder, he grumbled, 'look, my lord, we cannot save everyone. Our duty right now is to protect you and these women. The rest of the town will have to fend for themselves.'

His words cut through the tension, but I knew my mentor was right. We couldn't risk putting ourselves in danger while trying to save the whole town. Our focus lay on getting the bishop and the women out of Hereford and obtaining the ring. I took a deep breath. 'My lord bishop, if I may ask, have you somehow safeguarded the relic?'

He smiled, taking out the black box from his saddlebag. 'Of course, I wouldn't forget our arrangement, now would I?'

'Thank you, Lord,' I gasped, my fists balling at my side, my eyes now staring back to the road. We neared the last few streets leading out of town, but just as we turned the corner, two men on horseback blocked our way. I felt my mouth open – it was the bloody warrior and the hooded monk from Echternach.

Wearing a mail hauberk, the warrior just sat in his saddle, staring me down. He remained upright, unsheathing his sword as his eyes fixed on mine, his cheeks tensing. He wanted revenge, of that I was sure. Meanwhile, the monk finally removed his hood, revealing a long, gaunt face covered by a black tonsure, his eyes lingering on the black box in the bishop's hands.

'They must have rushed ahead of the Welsh army,' Trollmann spoke in a hushed tone. 'They probably chased us back into town, then circled around to block our exit to the south.'

The Echternach monk thought for a moment, then nodded at the warrior. The man's arms bulged beneath his armour as he stepped forward, his hand clutching his sword tightly. I stood frozen as the man raised his sword, letting out a fierce battle cry.

Before I could react, Robert suddenly screamed, lunging towards him. His sudden outburst caught us all off guard, and for a moment, we just stood there, stunned. However, Robert only had one arm to fight with, and it wasn't even his sword arm. He flung off his shield, wielding his blade in his left hand, hoping to catch our opponent off guard, but the six-foot-tall warrior swung his sword in Robert's direction.

My heart sank as I watched Robert battle the skilled warrior. Despite years of experience, Robert's injury was a disadvantage. The warrior's sword sliced through the air, with Robert struggling to parry the blows with his weaker arm.

'Trollmann, Frethirik, we have to help him,' I shouted. 'Come on!'

As we flew towards them, the two warriors clashed in a deadly dance, exchanging quick blows on horseback. While Robert fought valiantly, the warrior's strength was simply too great. With a powerful stroke, the warrior delivered a fatal blow to Robert's chest, and my mentor fell from his horse.

I cried out, my eyes streaming with tears. My mind shifted to our training sessions in Wiltenburg, to Robert's coarse jokes, and all of his fatherly advice over the past few months. I couldn't believe what just happened, my mentor lying lifelessly on the floor, his chest spouting with blood.

I pointed my sword up at the warrior. 'Leave the bastard to me, friends. His death is mine.' My cheeks heated up as I gritted my teeth, ready to exact revenge on that brute. The warrior now sneered back at me, charging forward. I took a deep breath and kicked the saddle, Winney rushing us towards him.

When the warrior approached me, I dodged his first blow, bowed left, and slashed my sword at his side. Using his shield, he parried the attack easily. I pressed on, using my horse's speed and agility to dodge his strikes and find an opening in his defense. I quickly realised he still relied entirely on his strength rather than speed.

We now circled each other, trading some blows and dodging attacks while I tried to find a weakness in his stance. As sweat streamed down my face, the warrior raised his blade for another powerful strike, crying out with the effort. I grinned. Too slow this time. I propelled myself forward, my sword ready.

In one fluid motion, I sliced his arm with precision. The warrior recoiled in pain, his arm dropping to his side. His eyes widened. I readied my sword. I had to kill him before he regained his senses for a counter-attack. Otherwise, it could mean my death.

Without another moment's hesitation, I bashed my shield into his chest with all the strength I could muster. With a fierce impact, his body shuddered as he tumbled from his horse, crashing into the dirt below with a loud thud. Writhing in pain, I knew he was finished, and he did too. My eyes locked onto his, now widening. He had underestimated my skill again, and now it would cost him his life. I was not about to show him any mercy after what he did to Robert.

I jumped at him, plunging my sword straight into the warrior's chest. He gasped, his eyes staring up at me. He coughed up some blood as he tried to utter some final words, but I even refused him that honour, silencing him with a final thrust to his heart. Panting and covered in sweat, I stood still for a moment before turning back to my companions.

Trollmann and Frethirik now hunched over Robert's side, their faces staring at the floor. I approached them slowly, my heart throbbing. As I looked at Robert's still form, my eyes welled. My mentor, my guide in life, now lay dead just like my father, and it had taken but the blink of an eye between his defiant charge and his heroic end. For a moment, I just froze, my body racked with sobs, my soul unable to comprehend the enormity of this loss.

Chapter Twenty-Eight

My moment of grief was short-lived, as Frethirik suddenly jumped up screaming, his eyes blazing. As he darted right past me, my eyes flickered to his target. The bishop lay on the ground, blood pouring from a knife wound in his side. The Echternach monk stood over him, grinning as he held the black box.

But then, as quickly as he had appeared, he turned and leapt onto his horse. The animal snorted and reared, its hooves striking sparks against the cobblestones, the monk fleeing into a nearby alleyway. As he disappeared into the distance, horns blared, followed by deafening cries from the north.

I shook my head, trying to clear my mind of the shock and confusion that gripped me. As I looked around, I saw that my friends were now on their feet, ready to face whatever came our way. Trollmann's eyes brow furrowed. 'They're coming, Reginhard,' he shouted. 'We must leave now. There's nothing we can do for Robert anymore.'

Shaken back to reality, I glanced at Robert once again. For a moment, I hesitated, unsure what to do next. While Trollmann was right about leaving, I couldn't abandon my mentor like this. I looked around for another option. 'No. I can't just leave him here!' I pointed at Robert's destrier. 'Frethirik, bring Robert's horse over here,' I requested. 'We'll hoist him onto it and take him with us.'

Despite the chaos surrounding us, I knew we had to do everything we could to grant Robert an honourable burial, so we worked quickly and then reverently placed Robert's lifeless body onto the horse.

We had to go now, I thought. I watched Bishop Æthelstan's burly monk unload a pile of possessions from a simple cart drawn by a mule. Once the monk had finished, he turned to the injured bishop. With great care and gentleness, he lifted the bishop from the ground to place him on the cart, cushioning him with blankets and pillows.

The bishop's face was pale and strained. I felt a pang of sympathy as I saw how the old man winced when placed on the cart. Yet the enemy's approach didn't allow us to check on his wounds. We knew we had to put as much distance between ourselves and the Welsh as possible.

Everyone ready, Ciara and Cwenhild led the way, setting a brisk pace. Frethirik and I followed close behind, my eyes scanning the surroundings for any signs of danger. The sound of horns and the distant cries of battle still echoed through the streets, the Welsh closing in on us.

Trollmann quickly fetched the Echternach warrior's horse, our group setting off towards the south, the safest direction we could take. We moved swiftly, our horses' hooves pounding hard against the cobblestones.

After exiting the town's southern periphery, we passed through fields and woods, leaving the sound of screams behind. As the setting sun broke through the clouds, smoke arose from Hereford. I now rode at the back of the group, my eyes on the horizon. In the distance, the silhouette of a group of riders appeared from town, their banners flapping in the wind. I knew we had to keep moving.

We pushed our horses harder, but despite our urgency, the wounded bishop and the elderly clerics slowed us down. We pulled the animals along by their reins, and I glanced back constantly, fearing the Welsh outriders coming after us. The weight of our burden was heavy, and we had no alternative but to move on for several miles. The further we got before nightfall, the safer.

Finally, we found a suitable place to rest, some ten miles from town. By now, the sun had almost disappeared from the horizon, and we knew it would be dark soon. We stood in a clearing in the woods, surrounded by dense foliage providing some cover. We built a small fire before throwing our weary bodies down to rest.

As we hunched around the fire, Trollmann was the first to speak up, his voice deep. 'With any luck, their riders won't venture out this far, as looting the town should be a more attractive course of action. I guess that in the morning we'll be able to venture on south before turning east to Gloucester.'

I nodded, too tired to even reply. I knew the dark would provide us with the cover we needed for now, but just to be sure, we took turns keeping watch. As the night wore on, bishop Æthelstan, still awake, suddenly gestured me towards him.

I knelt beside him, casting a glance at his deep wound. I doubted the old man would survive for long, but at least his monks did their best for him. They removed the dagger and put various herbs into the wound before bandaging it. Still, Bishop Æthelstan now looked hardly more than a skeleton, his hazy eyes almost set for the afterlife.

'Dear Frisian,' he smiled, holding my hand gently. 'When I asked for your help I never expected our whole town to fall, let alone your own companion giving his life for our war. In fact, when Bishop Æthelmær contacted me with an offer, I had already made up my mind to accept. Willibrord's ring deserves a place in your Wiltenburg. It's only fair.'

Bishop Æthelstan started coughing uncontrollably until the huge monk approached, placing a cup of water to his lips. 'Did you even know,' Bishop Æthelstan winced before continuing, 'that your bishop offered us each a full hundred pounds of silver for the ring? With such a huge amount to help our dioceses, we were already happy to accept, but then of course the Witan outlawed Earl Ælfgar, starting this war.'

Crossing himself, the bishop paused again, his hazy eyes now closed. 'Of course, I need that silver even more now. I'm sure there will be nothing left of my cathedral tomorrow.' He took another sip. 'A few days ago, I got a letter from Bishop Æthelmær that a group of Frisian settlers arrived in his land, bringing him the full amount of silver in good faith. I was to get my share in the coming days.'

I swallowed hard, the truth of the bishop's words taking a while to process. Did the bishop just say Wiltenburg offered him and Bishop Æthelmær two hundred pounds of silver? An astonishing amount.

Bishop Æthelstan brought a shaky hand into his pocket, slowly pulling out a gleaming object. As I looked closer, my heart began to pound wildly. It couldn't be what I was thinking, could it? But hadn't I seen the Echternach monk snatch it from us?

The bishop held out the object to me, and I realised it was indeed Willibrord's ring, glittering in all its magnificence. Overcome by its holiness, I slowly opened my hands.

'The ring is now yours to take back to Wiltenburg, young Frisian,' the bishop said softly. 'I'm sure your bishop will be honoured to receive it.'

As I stood there with the precious relic, Frethirik rushed over to my side, holding onto my shoulders. Once he fully understood what I held, he placed his fist over his mouth, a muffled grunt coming out. 'You got it, Reginhard,' he whispered, his eyes beaming with pride. 'This is what you were looking for all these weeks. By God, Bishop William will surely reward you now.'

Yet, as today's events came to mind again, my elation died as quickly as it had come. 'Yes, Frethirik, but the cost of Robert's life was never worth it,' I said, my stomach twisting. 'A man died for a noble cause, but for me, no cause could have been great enough to be worth his life. Not even two hundred pounds of bloody silver.'

Frethirik didn't reply, his head hanging low. Robert's tragic loss of life simply overshadowed the holiness of the ring. Never again could I talk, laugh or share drinks of fellowship with my mentor. While my mission neared completion, my mouth tasted sour, and my heart stung with the weight of his death. And at that moment, the sorrow from Veenkoop all those weeks ago rushed fully back to mind too.

Overcome with sadness, I collapsed in tears, my body convulsing with grief. At that moment, the weight of all my losses and sacrifices became too much to bear. Frethirik needed no words to understand my pain. He placed his hand on my shoulder to provide silent comfort on that cold and bitter night. I will never forget how, on that 24th of October, our greatest success hurt more than any wounds the Welsh had inflicted on us. Robert had died that day.

Epilogue

We reached Gloucester the next day, where Bishop Æthelstan finally received medical assistance. In the afternoon, we paid our respects to Robert with great honour as the bishop of Gloucester himself delivered a eulogy in his memory. The church provided a magnificently carved wooden cross inscribed with Robert's remarkable deeds and valiant sacrifice in service of the English. Hearing this news brought a tiny smile to my face. At least he was honoured in death.

After the burial, Trollmann stood by my side, holding Robert's destrier Storm by the reins. 'Here, Reginhard, you take this horse now. It will serve as a symbol of Robert's memory,' he said. I took the reins in silence. Although grateful for the gesture, my heart was still heavy with grief.

Unable to smile, I faced my friends, finally finding my voice. 'I have something for you too, Trollmann. You and Frethirik have stood by my side through thick and thin, and I want to show my gratitude,' I said, pointing at the stables, where the horse I had won from the Echternach warrior stood.

Trollmann raised his brow. 'That's a magnificent horse, Reginhard. It will fetch a good price in Gloucester, especially in these times of war, when horses are in high demand.' He took my hand. 'Thank you.'

Though this exchange of gifts felt bittersweet, it reminded me that even in times of sorrow, our friendship pushed us onward, and the solace of being together made me feel somewhat better.

Even though the loss of Robert weighed on our hearts, the comfort of being together and my comrades' support helped me focus on returning to Wiltenburg.

I knew we still had the formidable challenge of crossing the sea and returning Willibrord's ring to Bishop William. The sooner we got to Ipswich, the better our chances to sail, winter now approaching.

Frethirik's arm draped over my shoulder. As I straightened my posture, I found myself finally able to smile, knowing that Robert could now enjoy the eternal peace of Heaven. I glanced at my reins, and it was as if Robert's horse thought the same, neighing softly. I stroked his mane gently. 'I miss your master too, Storm, but Robert is better off now you know. We must now head to Ipswich as soon as we can.'

It hardly took Trollmann any effort to sell the warhorse. After a hushed conversation, the stable master rushed back with a fat purse, and I saw the Sami nod, shaking hands on the trade. Then Gerold and the girls joined our side for us to depart from Gloucester. We aimed to make a couple of miles that day and hoped to reach Ipswich before the start of November.

After six arduous days of travel, we stood in Ipswich's harbour, staring at Jan's ship. The captain's eyes lit up as we approached him, and he rushed towards us with open arms. He embraced each man fondly, his booming laughter echoing across the harbour, causing a flock of seagulls to take flight.

I had never seen Jan so emotional, and his joy at our safe return was infectious. As he hugged me, he exclaimed, 'Reginhard, my friend. You look like a true warrior now, with scars to match!' I grinned in response, suddenly feeling proud of the battles I survived. However, as he scanned the group, his smile turned sour when he noticed Ciara and Cwenhild standing beside us. Frowning, Jan inspected the girls from top to bottom, his eyes narrowing. 'What have you done, Frethirik? You better plan to marry one of them? I will not tolerate any indecency on my ship.'

Frethirik's stumbled over his response, his face turning beet red. 'Of course, Father. We plan to do so in Frisia. Please, allow me to introduce Cwenhild. And this is Ciara, now betrothed to Reginhard.'

In the meantime, the crew assembled around us, their eyes glittering. In total quiet, their gaze flashed from us to the girls and then back to their captain. Jan's glare bore straight into Frethirik's downcast face, Jan taking his sweet time. Then, as if nothing had happened, his cheeks relaxed, and he started chuckling. 'That's the right answer, son. Well, congratulations to you both.' Yet after Jan looked over the group again, his brow furrowed. 'Wait, but where is Robert?'

Trollmann stepped forward, explaining what happened, Jan's eyes filling with tears. 'Well, he met his end in glory then.' Jan swirled around, pointing at his ship. 'Rurik, fetch the mead. We toast on the death of a great warrior.' We all stood in silence for a moment, remembering the fallen warrior who had given his life to protect us. Then we raised our horns, my thoughts filled with grief and gratitude for the bonds of friendship that had seen us through even the darkest times.

We spent one more day in Ipswich, making preparations for our departure. The cog that had initially set sail with us to transport the Frisian settlers was now packed with our belongings, including Winney, Storm, and my trusty Welsh pony. Meanwhile, we boarded the Snekkja, ensuring everything was in order before setting sail.

On the first of November, greeted by a dark and misty dawn, we set out on our perilous journey. As the days passed, the weather grew colder and harsher, and we had to contend with ice forming on the deck and rigging. But we pressed on, now driven to return home to fulfill our duties. Finally, after three days of treacherous sailing, we spotted the familiar coastline of Starum in the distance.

We wasted no time while in Starum, and together with Jan, Trollmann, Frethirik, Gerold, and the women, we headed straight to Wiltenburg. Within a few days, we arrived on a chilly morning, snow covering the walls of the town.

Bishop William received us warmly in his chapel, his arms wide when we walked in. Wasting no time, I fell on my knee to present him with Willibrord's ring. He uttered a high-pitched cry, shouting to his servants that a feast was in order.

The success of our mission was widely celebrated in the afternoon as the entire town gathered to greet us, cheering for us in the streets. We feasted all day, a magnificent joust even organised in our honour. Seated next to the bishop as victorious spectators, I felt honoured when William announced me as the hero of Wiltenburg, waving his arm down for two warriors to start their joust.

I enjoyed every moment of the celebration, the luxury of the feast: expensive wine, honeyed cakes, salted pork ribs, and spiced duck – all a new experience. I had never felt prouder of my accomplishments than at that moment, my mind wondering about my father. Did he experience the same level of honour after he killed Count Dirk at Thuredrith?

After a resplendent evening, we were given a fabulous room in the bishop's residence, where I slept well until noon. Crawling to the barracks, we all had an ale together, telling our many tales to the warriors surrounding us. Yet before Frethirik could finish his flamboyant tale of overcoming the Ipswich bandits, we suddenly got interrupted by a servant summoning us to the bishop's tower. 'His Lordship summons you Reginhard, and your companions can come too.'

I could feel my pulse racing in my temples, my breaths coming in short, shallow gasps. Every beat of my heart felt like a drum pounding in my chest, drowning out all other sounds. I tried to calm myself, but my stomach twisted and turned. This was it then, the moment of my reward.

Everyone jumped to their feet, following me to the bishop's residence. When we arrived, a cold sweat broke out on my forehead, and my hands were clammy as I wiped them on my tunic. Fantastical thoughts raced through my mind, and I tried to focus on something, anything, to distract myself from the overwhelming nerves that consumed me.

The tower doors creaked open as a herald announced our arrival. I walked in, immediately overwhelmed by the sight in front of me. The bishop sat on his magnificent wooden chair adorned with intricate carvings that seemed to glow in the flickering light of the torches. Around him stood a group of priests in flowing white robes that marked them as members of the clergy. They spoke in hushed tones, their eyes focused on the bishop as he addressed them with a wide smile.

The bishop's usually stern features were now softened, his eyes sparkling with childlike delight. His arms stretched out when he spotted me, welcoming me closer. I passed warriors standing guard at the entrance to the hall, their weapons at the ready. Yet their eyes seemed relaxed and at ease. A festive atmosphere even permeated their stoic demeanor, and I saw one lad my age lick his lips.

The aroma of roasted meats and freshly baked bread mingled

with jovial conversation and the clinking of glasses. It was clear that this was a moment of celebration. While I observed the scene around me, I sighed deeply. This was it then. First, I bowed before getting down on one knee. It took me a while to find my voice. 'Hail Prince Bishop of Wiltenburg.'

He moved his hand towards me, and I kissed his ring. Then I felt him reach out to grasp my chin, gently pulling me up to a standing position. A forced smile covered his face. Once I stood before him, the bishop gestured towards a nearby table, where a beautifully crafted chest sat prominently on display. My gaze followed the bishop's outstretched arm until I realised that the open chest held Willibrord's ring, its presence filling the hall.

Despite the bishop's forced smile, I felt an underlying tension in the air, as if everyone present was acutely aware of the importance of the moment, everyone but me. As I looked around the room, the courtiers' eyes shone brightly.

Bishop William lifted his hand, gesturing for silence. It took a while, but the audience slowly stopped their chattering. The hall steadily grew still, all eyes turning towards the bishop as he prepared to speak. 'Reginhard,' he began, his deep voice carrying my name along the towering walls. 'All those gathered here today know of your remarkable deeds. Every servant of Wiltenburg by now has heard how you uncovered the holy relic of Saint Willibrord of Wiltenburg, the first bishop of our princedom.'

Men started cheering around me, clapping their hands and thundering their feet rhythmically on the floor until the bishop's hand urged for silence to return. As the bishop's words rang through me, I suppressed a shiver. As I scanned the audience, I noticed a deep admiration in the courtiers' faces. Despite my nerves, I straightened my back, proud to have played a role in this holy event.

'And so, as is proper for the completion of such a holy mission, I will reward you well,' the bishop declared, looking out over the assembly. Raising his voice, he continued, 'Reginhard, everyone in the bishopric was of course horrified by the actions of the criminal count of Holland, when he took your father's estate.'

The hall erupted in screams, the memory of that day hitting me hard. I swallowed, fighting back tears as the warriors around me protested wildly at the loss of my homeland. William posed like a statue, waiting for the men to calm down again. 'Unfortunately, we cannot undo this wrong right now,' he said, 'but we will always remember your claim to that land. And we promise to assist you in recapturing this property when possible.'

That caught me off guard. As I tried to process his words, my confusion deepened. What did he mean? If we would not try to take back Veenkoop, what reward would I receive instead?

After a brief pause, the bishop added, 'since no more ministerial lands are presently unoccupied I cannot grant you one in my domain. However in the bounty of my hospitality I will reward you with this chest of silver.'

A servant moved forward, opening a chest, and I gasped at the gleaming coins. I just couldn't believe my eyes. There had to be over five hundred pennies; worth at least five swords. Never before had I seen so much silver in one pile, let alone received it. I stepped forward to accept the chest with shaking hands, overwhelmed by the honour.

Glancing around, the courtiers whispered among themselves, giving me nods of approval. Some approached, offering congratulations and praise for my accomplishment, even though I couldn't help but notice some flickers of envy as I looked them in the eye.

I lifted the heavy chest, struggling to keep a grip on its weight.

A surge of satisfaction washed over me, knowing that my hard work had not gone unnoticed. Still, a pang of guilt hit me at the memory of Robert's death. Despite this success, I couldn't shake the feeling that it had come at too great a cost.

To everyone's surprise, Bishop William wasn't even finished yet. He raised his hands once more. 'Of course, young Reginhard, your services to the English have not gone unnoticed either. As all here are aware, I sent a dozen families along with Reginhard to England as part of an arrangement I made with the Bishop of Elmsham.'

William smiled as he continued. 'Bishop Æthelmaer was greatly impressed by your heroic rescue of Bishop Æthelstan of Hereford.' He paused, aware of the excitement he had created, waiting for another wave of applause to die down. 'Instead of appointing an English thegn to oversee his new colony of Frisian settlers, he asked for you, Reginhard.'

The room now turned stone silent. The only thing I heard at that point was my heart pounding in my chest and the bated breathing of the courtiers as they took in this information. But the bishop just continued as if it was all a matter of course. 'Even though you are exceptionally young, not even twenty summers old, you proved your worth when you came back for the bishop, braving the Welsh to regain Willibrord's ring. That proves you are loyal to Wiltenburg and brave in the face of danger, everything we look for in a ministerial. What's more, you were raised one and taught to oversee clearance projects.'

Bishop William raised a hand. 'Reginhard, you are hereby appointed Thegn of Friston, the name of the new Frisian settlement in East Anglia. You have my blessing to lead our people there and enter the service of the English church.'

All eyes shifted from the bishop back to me. My heart raced as I tried to process what the bishop just said. Becoming a thegn in England, overseeing a colony of Frisian settlers, was beyond my wildest dreams. I thought back on my father. What would he have said now? How proud would he be?

I sighed, thrilled to my core. Familiar with colonising peatland, I knew how to build farms from scratch. Of course, my father had always been right to train me as an overseer all these years, and I knew I was up to the job. I had come so far from the simple life I had known as a young boy in Veenkoop, and now I was being given this incredible opportunity. Around me, the courtiers chatted amongst themselves again, no doubt speculating on the implications of this announcement.

I looked back at Bishop William, my throat suddenly dry. 'Thank you, Your Grace,' I managed to mutter, my voice barely above a whisper. 'I am honoured to accept this appointment and to serve the English church from here on.'

As soon as I uttered these words, it was as if a giant burden had been lifted. I glanced at Jan, Frethirik, Trollmann, Gerold, Ciara, and Cwenhild, their faces lighting up. Without hesitation, they rushed up to me, beaming as they congratulated me, each embracing me fondly. For a moment, I felt like a hero who had accomplished something remarkable. And as I basked in all this adulation, I knew my journey had been worth it. Willibrord's ring was safely restored to Wiltenburg, I had the finest woman a young man could dream of, and even my father's rank now passed to me; fate had decided, and for now, it favoured me.

But when the excitement began to die, a sobering thought began to take hold of me. I realised that my new role as Thegn of

Friston would also bring many challenges. Thinking back on our journey in England, I knew one never had to wait long for war to arrive in that land, and once it did, I had to be ready. Besides, I thought, gritting my teeth, I certainly hadn't forgotten about Count Floris and Ragnar Ivarson. But then I shook my head. That was all to be dealt with later.

Bishop William now raised a silver chalice high in the air. 'Let us toast then. On the return of Willibrord's ring.' As we all raised our cups and cheered, I couldn't help but reflect on the journey that had brought me to this moment. From a young boy dreaming of adventure to a man who had lived through battles and perilous missions, I had finally found my place in the world.

I looked around the room at the faces of my friends and allies, feeling grateful for their companionship. And as the night wore on and the wine flowed, I knew this moment would stay with me forever, a memory of a time when I had truly lived.

Historical Note

This story is based on factual evidence, beginning in the mid-eleventh century and crossing between two countries: Frisia and England. The main idea is to show the rich, multicultural medieval world through the eyes of the main character, Reginhard. Of course, the more prominent figures, such as kings and, below them, the earls, did actually exist. Facts based on their policies and actions came from various sources, which I have included below.

Yet, I used imagination, where sources lacked detail, to delve into the world a commoner lived through during the reign of King Edward the Confessor. The main character, Reginhard, is from a ministerial family, something precursing a landed knight. Not many records exist on individual ministerials, so I invented Veenkoop, placing it where the town of s-Gravendeel stands today, not far from the village where I was born. The county that was just becoming known as Holland originated between Thuredrith (modern-day Dordrecht) and Flardingas (modern-day Vlaardingen), its borderlands hotly disputed between the Count of Holland and the Bishop of Wiltenburg (modern-day Utrecht).

So, while the village of Veenkoop did not exist, the town near it, Thuredrith did. Still, I imagined this village as something that could have existed – built there in the great clearance of land that started in the eleventh century. Dykes were built and colonists ventured out to farm new lands, clearing the peat to graze sheep there. This process enabled Holland and Frisia to become increasingly more populated, allowing them to extend their power (something Holland was eventually able to do best.)

I took the basis of the great battles in the book from primary sources, such as the Anglo-Saxon Chronicles, which describe how Earl Ralph fled from the field at Hereford and the Welsh burned his castle, its cathedral having to be entirely rebuilt. These sources also mention how Bishop Æthelstan died not long after, although he did survive the looting of his church.

Friston existed back in 1055 and still exists today. The name means basically 'dwellings of Frisians.' In other words, it was a small colony of settlers in England, East Anglia. Back then, all of modern Holland was still called Frisia, and its inhabitants were a strange mix of people who were influenced by both the Frankish world (modern-day Germany that it was then a part of) and an older tribal one (which was more comparable to the Scandinavian Viking culture.)

The idea of the characters is that they envision their world, not ours, and so their morals are far removed from what we deem correct. Slavery, for one, is seen as acceptable by them, in this context called thralldom, while slaughtering and ruling over innocents is not uncommon to them either.

To understand the context of the time in more detail, I recommend not only reading about it but seeing it. There is a fantastic village called West Stow Anglo-Saxon Village (in Suffolk, England), where you can see an Anglo-Saxon village from the Middle Ages. When I visited, there were enthusiastic reenactors (by the name of Swords of Penda) who showed us everything from armour to combat styles of the early medieval battlefield, some aspects of which I used for the story itself.

Writing historical fiction requires a balance between fact and fiction. I tried to show you realistic medieval characters and their thoughts. Yet, I also wanted to show the various aspects that made up their life, from food to interiors, armour to weapons, and battles to castles. Of course, it is possible my scenes may be looked at differently later in time. We must always accept that many parts of medieval life are subject to interpretation rather than factual evidence, and interpretations change over time as more and more information from literature, archeology or even linguistics shed new light on the Middle Ages.

Thank you for reading 'The Frisian.' I hope you enjoyed it because Reginhard's adventure is not yet finished.

Glossary

Cog: A high boat that started to replace older Knarrs. It was built to carry both cargo but still ride high in the water to be effective in the Frisian rivers, where a captain did not want to get stuck.

Earl: A nobleman of significant status below the king. These were the men with the real power in the medieval world, and they usually had high offices, assisted the king in ruling and making decisions, and controlled large amounts of land.

Gambeson: A padded jacket that needed to be worn beneath mail protection. It could also be worn separately and offered some protection against medieval weapons.

Knarr: A Norse trading vessel. It was broad and not particularly fast, although it could carry significant cargo.

Mail: Mail could be shaped into either a hauberk (long) or a shirt (shorter) and consisted of various interlocking rings. The hauberks tended to be long and were worn from shoulder to knee. The shirt was usually shorter and was worn from shoulder to waist.

Seax: A short sword introduced by the Saxons. In fact, it is what gave this tribe their name, and it could be worn by all free men. It was a standard weapon suitable for creating a shieldwall, where a warrior could stab another in unprotected parts where little space made the seax very practical.

Snekkja: A Viking longship, usually a warship. It was thin and long and was known for its speed.

Thegn: A minor nobleman below an earl. It was the eleventh-century version of the English gentry.

Teulu: The Welsh version of retinue, or followers of a lord. These professional soldiers were seen as the bodyguard of a lord.

Thrall: The Anglo-Saxon version of slave. Usually, these were captured in raids and were traded everywhere around the North Sea.

Bibliography

Aalbers, J. etc. Geschiedenis van de Provincie Utrecht tot 1528. Utrecht, Het Spectrum: 1997. 67-179. Print

A Late Saxon Village and Medieval Manor: Excavations at Botolph Bridge, Orton Longueville, Peterborough

The Anglo-Saxon Chronicle. Eds. Giles, J. A. (John Allen) 1808-1884 Translator; Ingram, J. (James) 1774-1850 Translator. Project Gutenburg. 1996. Ebook.

Annalen van Egmond. Eds. Gumbert-Hepp, M., Gumbert, J., en Burgers, J.W.J. Hilversum: Verloren, 2007, Print.

Barlow, Frank. *Edward the Confessor.* Eyre Methuen. 1979. Print.

Bartlett, Robert. *The Making of Europe: Conquest, Colonization and Cultural Change 950-1350.* London: Penguin Books, 1994. Print.

Blockmans, Wim. *Metropolen aan de Noordzee: De Geschiedenis van Nederland, 1100- 1560.* Amsterdam: Uitgeverij Bert Bakker, 2012. 9-195. Print.

Blockmans, Wim and Peter Hoppenbrouwers. *Introduction to Medieval Europe 300-1500.* London: Routledge, 2007. Print.

De Boer, D.E.H. and E.H.P. Cordfunke. *Graven van Holland: Portretten in Woord en Beeld (880-1580).* Zutphen: Walburg Pers, 1995. 26-31. Print.

Brooks, N. "The Social and Political Background." The Cambridge Companion to Old English Literature. Eds. Malcolm Godden, and Michael Lapidge. Cambridge: Cambridge University Press, 2013. 1–18. Print.

Brown, N. Jennifer. "Body, Gender and Nation in the Lives of Edward the Confessor." *Barking Abbey and Medieval Literary Culture: Authorship and Authority in a Female Community.* Eds. Donna Alfano Bussell and Jennifer N. Brown. York: Boydell & Brewer, York medieval Press, 2012. 145– 163. Print.

Brownworth, Lars. *The Normans: From Raiders to Kings.* Crux Publishing. 2014. Ebook.

Campbell, J. *The Anglo Saxons.* London: Penguin Books, 1991. Print.

Clarke, Howard B., Sheila Dooley, and Ruth Johnsen. *Dublin and the Viking World.* Dublin: The O'Brien Press, 2018. Print.

Crumlin-Pedersen, Ole. "To be or not to be a cog: the Bremen Cog in perspective." *The International Journal of Nautical Archaeology* 29:2 (2000): 230–246. Print.

Davies, Michael and Sean Davies. *The Last King of Wales: Gruffudd ap Llywelyn c. 1013-1063.* Cheltenham, the History Press. 2012. Ebook.

Davies, Sean. *War and Society in Medieval Wales, 633-1283.* Cardiff: The University of Wales Press, 2004. Ebook.

Dronkers, Jaap etc. *Adel en Ridderschap in Gelderland: Tien Eeuwen Geschiedenis.* Arnhem: WBooks, 2013.13-24. Print.

Gerald of Wales : Instruction for a Ruler (De Principis Instructione). Ed. Bartlett, Robert. Oxford, Oxford University Press, 2018. Print.

De Graaf, Ronald Peter. *Oorlog om Holland 1000-1300.* Diss. University of Groningen, Groningen, 1996. 19-207. Print.

Graham-Campbell, James. *The Viking World.* London: Quarto Publishing, 2013. Print.

Van Herwaarden, Jan etc. *De Geschiedenis van Dordrecht tot 1572.* Hilversum: Uitgeverij Verloren, 1996. 15-21. Print.

Janse, A. *Ridderschap in Holland.* Hilversum: Uitgeverij Verloren, 2001. Print.

Mack, Katharin. "Changing Thegns: Cnut's Conquest and the English Aristocracy." *Albion: A Quarterly Journal Concerned with British Studies* 16:4 (1984): 375–387. Print.

Morris, Marc. *The Norman Conquest.* Hutchinson, 2012. Ebook.

Oorkondenboek van het Sticht Utrecht. Eds. A.C. Bouman and S. Muller. Utrecht: van Kemink & Zoon, 1920. 189-214. Print.

Oorkondenboek van het sticht Utrecht tot 1301. Ed. Bouman. Utrecht: Oosthoek, 1920. Print.

Peers, Chris. *The Highland Battles: Warfare on Scotland's Northern Frontier in the Early Middle Ages.* Pen and Sword Military, 2020. Ebook.

Price, Neil. *De Vikingen: Een Nieuwe Geschiedenis.* Translator: Roelof Posthuma. Nieuw Amsterdam, 2020. Ebook.

Roesdahl, Else. *The Vikings.* Tr. Susan M. Margeson, and Kirsten Williams. Penguin Books, 2016.

Tyler, Elizabeth M. *Crossing Conquests: Polyglot Royal Women and Literary Culture in Eleventh Century England, Conceptualizing Multilingualism in England, c.800-c.1250.* Ed. Elizabeth M. Tyler. Turnhout, Brepols Publishers, 2011. 171–196. Print.

Tyler, Elizabeth M. *Introduction England and Multilingualism: Medieval and Modern, Conceptualizing Multilingualism in England, c.800-c.1250.* Ed. Elizabeth M. Tyler. Turnhout, Brepols Publishers, 2011. 1–14. Print.

Van der Linde, H. *De Cope. Een Bijdrage tot de Rechtsgeschiedenis van de Openlegging der Hollands-Utrechtse Laagvlakte.* Assen, van Gorcum, 1981. Print.

Van de Ven, G.P. *Leefbaar Laagland. Geschiedenis van de Waterbeheersing en Landaanwinning in Nederland.* Utrecht: Matrijs, 2003. Print.

Van Winter, J.M. "De Opkomst van Ministrialiteit en Ridderschap." *Geschiedenis Utrecht.* Ed. C. Dekker.

Williams, Brenda. *The Normans.* Pitkin Publishing, 2002. Ebook.

Williams, Brian. *Life in a Medieval Castle.* The Mill, Brimscombe Port Stroud: Pitkin Publishing. 2013. Ebook.

Williams, Gareth. *The Viking Ship.* London: The British Museum Press. 2014. Print.

Williams, Thomas. *Viking Britain.* London: William Collins. 2017. Print.

Woodman, David. *Edward the Confessor. The Sainted King.* Penguin Books. 2020. Ebook.

Websites:

Jessie M. Lyons Source: PMLA , 1918, Vol. 33, No. 4 (1918), pp. 644-655 Published by: Modern Language Association Stable URL:

- www.jstor.org/stable/456984

- friston.OneSuffolk.net/home/history/

- ReadingMuseum.org.uk/collections/britains-bayeux-tapestry

Acknowledgments

While spending many hours researching medieval history is a rather individual chore, I couldn't have finished this book without the help of so many around me.

First, I would like to thank my family and friends, who gave me priceless feedback as the novel progressed.

Thanks also go to my father, who accompanied me on my research trip to England, and who had to endure endless discussions concerning Anglo-Saxon England.

Yet special thanks go to my writer's group and especially my mentor, Suzanne, who taught me so much about writing, and made me believe in my novel from the start.

About the Author

Richard van der Ven was born in Holland near the town of Dordrecht and studied medieval literature at Leiden University. Here his fascination on 11th century medieval society began in earnest.

The Frisian: The Legacy of Willibrord is his first novel.

RichardVanDerVen.com

Printed in Dunstable, United Kingdom